"Are you

"I've acquired a few answered. His gaze like a sweet caress

ng

Katrina blinked, shifting away from the emotion rising between them. "Everything is so massive," she noted as her gaze wafted from one work of art to another.

"That's how we do things here in Texas, ma'am," Matthew said, exaggerating his deep Southern drawl. "We breed everything big down here!"

She laughed, her head waving from side to side. "You are so *not* funny," she said as she rolled her eyes.

He pulled her hand to his lips and kissed the back of it. The sensation was electric, causing Katrina to gasp loudly. "That's why you laughed." Matthew grinned. "Are you ready for dinner, Judge Broomes?"

"Is that going to be big, too?"

Matthew took a step toward her, moving his body near to hers. Katrina felt herself holding her breath at the nearness of him. His fingers gently caressed the length of her arm as he spoke.

"I hope it will exceed your expectations," Matthew said, his gentle tone soothing. "I'm hoping this whole evening is going to be an event like nothing you've ever experienced before. If that takes big, then I assure you it will be the biggest meal you will ever have."

Easing her gaze up to meet his, Katrina suddenly wanted to kiss the full lips smiling down at her. The heat from his body had ignited a flame deep in her midsection and she suddenly felt like she might combust from the intensity of it. She fought the sensation.

Her voice was barely a whisper as she responded. "I'd say you're off to a good start," she said softly.

DEBORAH FLETCHER MELLO

Writing since she was thirteen years old, Deborah Fletcher Mello can't imagine herself doing anything else. Her first romance novel, *Take Me To Heart*, earned her a 2004 Romance Slam Jam nomination for Best New Author. In 2005, she received Book of the Year and Favorite Heroine nominations for her novel *The Right Side of Love*, and in 2009 won an *RT Book Reviews* Reviewer's Choice Award for her ninth novel *Tame a Wild Stallion*. Most recently, Deborah's eleventh novel, *Promises to a Stallion*, has earned her a 2011 Romance Slam Jam nomination for Hero Of The Year.

For Deborah, writing is as necessary as breathing, and she firmly believes that if she could not write, she would cease to exist. Weaving a story that leaves her audience feeling full and complete, as if they've just enjoyed an incredible meal, is an ultimate thrill for her. Born and raised in Connecticut, Deborah now maintains base camp in North Carolina but considers home to be wherever the moment moves her.

Seduced

BY A

STALLION

Deborah Fletcher Mello

KIMANI
ROMANCE

To my grandmother, Mrs. Susie M. Cole,
Your spirit continues to amaze and delight.
You are my inspiration and I love you beyond words.

 KIMANI PRESS™

ISBN-13: 978-0-373-86258-0

SEDUCED BY A STALLION

Copyright © 2012 by Deborah Fletcher Mello

PLEASE RECYCLE
THIS PRODUCT IS RECYCLABLE

Recycling programs
for this product may
not exist in your area.

www.kimanipress.com

Printed in U.S.A.

Dear Reader,

It seems like it took forever, but the Stallion men are finally back! Those billionaire brothers, Matthew, Mark, Luke and John Stallion are back and they are bigger and better than ever with brother Matthew's story. A definite Stallion stud, Matthew does not disappoint as he meets his match in district court judge Katrina Broomes.

I absolutely loved writing Matthew's story. With each brother's unique personality, conservative attorney Matthew brought a whole new dynamic to the table with everyone dying to know if he fathered family friend Vanessa Long's baby. Is Matthew the father of Vanessa's baby? Does Vanessa bring the baby-mama drama into Matthew and Katrina's relationship?

Seduced By a Stallion answers those questions and opens the doors to much, much more to come. It was so much fun to write and I know you won't be disappointed!

As always I have to thank each of you for taking this amazing journey with me. None of this would be possible if it were not for your support. Your words of encouragement, your critiques and your criticisms continue to keep me writing and always motivate me to write well.

I always love to hear what you think so please, please, please contact me at DeborahMello@aol.com.

Until the next time, take care and God bless.

With much love,

Deborah Fletcher Mello
www.DeborahMello.blogspot.com

Chapter 1

Chaos reigned at the Dallas County courthouse. Loud whispers echoed from one end of each hallowed hall to the other. Matthew Stallion avoided the crowds and entered the building through the employee entrance, a privilege afforded him by his Harvard law degree. Although he hadn't practiced criminal law since the year after he passed the state's bar exam, he had spent much time in the courthouse navigating civil suits for his family's business. Stallion Enterprises, which had been his older brother John's brainchild, was a successful corporate empire built on commercial real estate and development, as well as a shipping company with numerous entertainment interests.

As the door locked securely behind him, he pulled at the lapels of his business suit, adjusting the silk jacket neatly against his solid frame. The charcoal-gray against the bright white dress shirt and his raspberry-colored tie flattered his mahogany complexion nicely.

Sticking his head into the county clerk's office, he greeted the two women bustling around inside, the duo getting ready for what was already proving to be a very busy day in the Dallas judicial system.

"Good morning, ladies," Matthew said with a wide grin.

Mrs. Nettie Banks grinned back. "Good morning, Counselor. How are you faring this beautiful morning?"

"No complaints," Matthew answered.

The other woman, Mrs. Maxine Bright, nodded. "No one listens when you do complain, baby." She chuckled softly, shifting a folder of paperwork from one desk to another.

"What brings you here this morning, Mr. Stallion?" Mrs. Banks asked, a look of confusion crossing her face. "I don't remember seeing that you had filed for anything recently."

"I didn't. I was subpoenaed to family court and thought I'd take a minute to come say hello to you two lovely ladies."

Both women eyed him suspiciously.

Matthew laughed warmly, lifting both his hands up as if in surrender. "I swear," he said with a deep chuckle. "I didn't do anything. Some kid stole my car. I don't even know why it's in family court and not over in the criminal building."

Mrs. Bright shook her head, laughing with him. "You had us worried for a hot minute there, Attorney Stallion."

Mrs. Banks nodded. "A hot minute," she echoed as she flipped through a clipped stack of papers. "There you are. You're seeing Judge Tyler this morning." She continued to browse through her notes, her expression stern. "This is that case with Judge Broomes's son. That's probably why they moved it to family. He's one of ours."

Matthew nodded, his curiosity suddenly raised. "Who's Judge Broomes?"

"Judge Katrina Broomes. The governor appointed her to replace the late Judge Harris. She hasn't been with us long," Mrs. Bright responded.

"Katrina? So, Judge Broomes is a woman?"

"We do have female judges, Counselor," Mrs. Bright said, her hands dropping to her full hips.

"Yes, ma'am, I know. I was just asking," he said with a soft chuckle.

The woman tossed him a warm smile, gesturing toward the large clock on the wall behind her. "Well, you better head on up. Judge Tyler doesn't take kindly to court starting late."

"Thank you, ladies. You two have a good day now," Matthew replied, tossing them both a wink of his eye.

As he walked out the door, the two women stared after him, both admiring the sway of his fit physique. When the door was closed securely behind him, Mrs. Banks shook her gray head from side to side. "Mmm, mmm, mmm. If I was twenty years younger," she said with a soft giggle.

"Honey, hush yo' mouth!" Mrs. Bright giggled with her. "Just hush yo' mouth!"

Matthew shook hands with the state prosecutor, a short, balding man with a bad comb-over of bright red hair. "Ed, good morning! How are you doing?"

"I'm doing well, sir. It's good to see you again. You were subpoenaed today, weren't you?"

"Yes, the State versus Collin Broomes. Kid stole my car."

"We're actually going to try to mediate that one. The boy is a judge's son. First offense, good family, ready to admit guilt. We're hoping to keep him out of the system and put him back on the right track. That is, of course, if you're amenable."

Matthew nodded. "Everything's negotiable, Ed."

"Good. Once the judge calls the court to order, I'll ask that you all be referred to the family mediator and I'll get you out as quickly as I can."

"Thank you," Matthew said, moving to take the seat directly behind the prosecutor.

He looked around the room. The crowd gathering was a hodgepodge of personalities, people from all social and economic walks of life. He couldn't begin to identify which of the sons sitting beside his mother was the son who had taken his Mercedes and had crashed it into the center median on Interstate 35. He couldn't, because there were far too many young boys sitting in that courtroom, waiting for their cases to be heard. The absurdity of that fact weighed heavily on his spirit. Matthew heaved a deep sigh.

Minutes later, with court officially in session, the court officer called the young man's name. "The State of Texas versus Collin Broomes!"

Matthew looked up just as young Collin walked to the front of the courtroom, his attorney leading the way. The lanky teenager stood in the vicinity of six feet tall. His over-size stature belied his baby face, and it was obvious that he wasn't quite comfortable with his height, that his maturation had not yet caught up with his size. He was neatly groomed, with a fresh haircut, khaki slacks, a navy blue polo shirt and leather loafers. With the exception of his hunched shoulders and the hands pushed deep into the pockets of his slacks, he didn't seem to fit in with the other young boys, with their baggy pants, T-shirts and overpriced sports shoes.

Matthew looked around for a parent but saw no one that resembled the child, nor anyone that looked ready to claim him. His thoughts were interrupted as Judge Tyler called his name.

"Attorney Stallion, are you in agreement with the State that this case would be better served with mediation?"

Matthew came to his feet, buttoning his suit jacket as he approached the bench. "I am, Your Honor. But under the circumstances, if the court permits, I would appreciate the opportunity to participate in those negotiations."

The judge nodded. "Not a problem, Counselor. The court will hold this case pending the outcome of mediation."

The young man met Matthew's eyes and stared. For most of the proceedings he'd looked disinterested. The judge calling Matthew's name had caught Collin's attention and he eyed Matthew curiously. When his attorney finally gestured with his head for Collin to follow, the boy did so, but not before looking back over his shoulder for one last look at the imposing black man.

Chapter 2

Katrina Broomes stood with her arms folded over her chest. Her right foot, sheathed in a patent-leather pump, tapped anxiously at the tiled floor. Every fiber of her body was annoyed. Katrina was still perturbed that, instead of being home on her one day off from work, she was pacing the hallway of family court, waiting for the disposition of her fifteen-year-old son's criminal case.

She blew a heavy sigh, warm breath pushing past her thin lips. She still couldn't believe that any child of hers was actually facing criminal charges. It was difficult to fathom that stupidity had seeped into her son's pores and had laid claim to his brain. This was not how she had raised her only child, a youngster intent on taxing her last good nerve with every foolish antic he could muster up.

She began to pace again, gliding from one end of the narrow hallway to the other. She'd been a single parent since forever, raising her baby boy by her lonesome. Her husband, Colonel Jackson Broomes, an army helicopter pilot, had been killed during the Gulf War. The day that he'd been deployed to active duty, she'd promised him that she would do whatever it took to ensure the safety and security of his family. She'd assured him that he wouldn't have to worry about his son, or her, while he was gone. She was still keeping that promise, still committed to doing whatever it took to keep her baby boy safe and sound, the way his father would have wanted.

Now her baby boy was a burgeoning young man, fast approaching adulthood, and keeping him safe was proving to be quite the challenge. When the boy was born, he'd come fighting his way into the world, kicking and screaming. Drawn to drama and commotion, Collin still hadn't learned how to settle down and relax in his own silence.

She turned abruptly when she heard her name being called.

"Thank you for waiting, Judge Broomes," the overpriced attorney she'd hired said, moving to her side. "We're meeting upstairs. The mediator has already gone ahead. Judge Tyler has given permission for the victim to participate in the negotiations, as well."

Katrina raised an eyebrow. "For what reason?"

"You may have heard of him. Matthew Stallion is a licensed attorney practicing law here in Dallas. He also heads the Briscoe Ranch Mentoring Foundation, which works with at-risk youth. He has a vested interest in seeing young men turn their lives around for the good. I think it would be to Collin's benefit to have him present, which is why I asked for his participation."

Katrina nodded. Matthew Stallion's reputation had definitely preceded him. Knowing that her first encounter with the man would not be under the best of circumstances further soured her mood. She blew a deep sigh. "That's fine." She caught her son's eye and shook her head, her annoyance registered all over her face.

Collin rolled his eyes skyward, knowing better than to say anything at all. The two followed behind their attorney as he headed in the direction of the elevator and the mediation rooms on the upper level of the courthouse.

Matthew and the state-appointed mediator, a young woman with crystal-blue eyes, a luxurious mane of blond hair and a wide smile, stood in conversation when they entered the room. The woman was giggling softly at something Matthew had just said, a full blush painting her pale complexion. Matthew was leaning in close, just a hair away from being too close, as he held the woman's full attention. As the trio stepped into the space, the woman jumped as if she'd been caught with her hand in the cookie jar. Clearly flustered by the male attention she'd been enjoying, the woman fought to gather her composure. She smiled politely as she gestured for them all to come in and find a seat, a manicured hand extended in greeting.

Behind her, Matthew Stallion pulled himself up to attention, securing his suit jacket around his frame. His dark eyes skated across the room, dancing over the other attorney and his client as they stared back with interest. Matthew's gaze was suddenly drawn to the exquisite woman who'd entered the room last. There was no mistaking the familial similarities between her and young Mr. Broomes. The boy had his mother's eyes, large dark orbs with forest-thick lashes that curled effortlessly. Energy vibrated from her stare as their gazes met and held. A smile pulled at Matthew's full lips, his expression showing much more than the fact that he was intrigued.

From where she stood at the entrance to the room, Katrina couldn't help but notice the handsome black man. She instinctively knew who he was, Matthew Stallion, the victim, the man whose car her son had stolen for a joyride. Matthew Stallion, of the prestigious Stallion family. He was a man of great wealth, was highly respected in the community and was considered one of Dallas's more eligible bachelors.

She found herself held hostage by the intense look that he was giving her, his eyes still locked with hers. Everyone else in the room seemed to vanish as the man stepped toward her, his engaging smile drawing her in like a spider might lure dinner into its web.

He extended his hand. "Good morning. I'm Matthew Stallion. It's a pleasure to meet you," he said, the deep bass in his tone reverberating warmly.

Katrina took a deep breath, air catching in her chest as his hand grazed hers, his firm grip holding tightly to her fingers. She tilted her head in greeting, words failing her. The other attorney came to her rescue without even realizing it.

"Counselor, this is Judge Katrina Broomes. Judge Broomes serves the Two Hundred Thirty-Second District Criminal Court. And this young man is Judge Broomes's son, Collin."

Matthew was still holding tight to Katrina's hand. Her son tossed him an uneasy smile, his hands still pushed deep into his pockets. With some reluctance, Matthew released Katrina's hand and extended his handshake to her child.

"I've been looking forward to meeting the young man who jacked my car," Matthew said, humor in his gaze. "What do you have to say for yourself?"

Collin's uneasy smile folded into a deep frown as he returned Matthew's handshake with much reluctance. "I'm very sorry," he managed to mutter softly.

Matthew nodded his head slowly, his gaze shifting from Collin to his mother and back again. He crossed his arms over his chest as he leaned back against the desktop. "Where did you learn to pop a door lock and hot-wire a car?"

Collin's eyes flitted to his mother's questioning expression, then back to the man who was studying him intently. "My friend Paul's older brother."

Matthew nodded again. "We need to work on getting you better friends," he said with a soft chuckle.

The boy suddenly looked scared.

Concern registered in Matthew's expression as a consoling smile filled his face. He tossed an arm around the boy's shoulder, patting him on his back. "I promise, you won't suffer much," Matthew said teasingly, winking his eye. His smile widened. "Why don't we all take a seat and see how we might fix this mess?" he said.

Following his lead, Katrina took a seat at the far end of the table. Matthew, quite the gentleman, pulled out her chair for her. She sat back, falling into silence as she stared from her son to Matthew and to the people around the table, trying to make sense of her child's actions. Her gaze kept returning to Matthew Stallion as he engaged her son in conversation, asking question after question about his life and his goals. Every so often Matthew would look in her direction, tossing her an easy smile before returning his focus to the matter at hand.

Katrina heaved a deep sigh, then inhaled deeply, holding tight to the warm air to calm her nerves. It was a good thing she was there only to observe, she suddenly mused. Katrina was unnerved by her reaction to the beautiful man who'd taken full control of the meeting. Unnerved because not since her late husband had any man had her quivering so unabashedly.

Chapter 3

Matthew engaged the voice-activation system in his car to dial his office. Traffic was backed up from Avery Avenue to Zang Boulevard. He strummed his fingers anxiously against the steering wheel of his new car as he waited for the cellular service to connect the call.

Mediation had lasted well over two hours. After their initial interaction, Collin Broomes hadn't been much interested in talking, falling into a sullen silence for the balance of the session. His attorney and the mediator had both been diligent about hashing out a game plan for the young man's future. But Matthew had been the only one to actually ask the boy his opinion, genuinely interested in what Collin might want for himself.

He'd hardly been surprised when Collin gave him little to nothing, his responses amounting to single-syllable answers. His mother had spoken only once during the entire discussion, reprimanding her son and advising him to check his tone when he became insolent. The boy had reeked of attitude, had a massive chip resting square on his shoulder. Her tone had been firm, the look she'd given her son stern. The boy had instantly stopped posturing, his teenage swagger cooling considerably. Clearly, his mother was a firm disciplinarian.

Each time she'd looked at Matthew, her gaze had lingered longer than necessary. Her look had softened considerably as she'd studied him with keen interest. Her eyes were beautiful, Matthew suddenly mused, remembering the glazed stare.

Matthew liked how Katrina Broomes had looked at him. He liked the energy that had pierced his own stare. Never had any woman looked at him like that before. Most women Matthew knew were always eyeing him like he was bait on a hook. But then, maybe that had much to do with him always trolling for his next catch of the moment.

On the other hand, Katrina had looked at him as if she actually saw something in him that he himself hadn't yet discovered. And she'd looked at him as though she liked what that was. Her interest had been keen and had piqued his. Now he found himself hoping that he might get to know the woman better.

Toward that goal he'd been eager to volunteer to personally mentor young Collin. The boy's eyebrows had risen in surprise but Matthew had been adamant. Consequently, starting in two weeks, the two would be meeting at the Briscoe Ranch Youth Center, where Matthew would put the child through his paces.

Matthew's thoughts were interrupted by the phone line being answered on the other end, his secretary's voice greeting him cheerfully.

"Matthew Stallion's office. How may I help you?"

"Hello, Carol. Do I have any messages?"

"Hello, Mr. Stallion. Just one message, sir. Your brother John asked that you contact him before you take off on your vacation this afternoon. He said he'll be in his office most of the day."

Matthew nodded into the receiver. "I'm actually changing my plans, Carol. If you'll call and cancel my reservations, please."

"But you were so looking forward to your vacation. Are you sure?" she asked, her tone concerned.

Matthew smiled to himself. "Positive. Something's come up."

There was a slight pause as his secretary waited, hopeful that Matthew might tell her what that something was. He didn't.

"I'm going to take the rest of the day off, though, and I'll be in the office tomorrow. If you'll please transfer me to John's office."

"Yes, sir, Mr. Stallion. Just one moment," Carol said as she put the call on hold.

Seconds later, John Stallion's baritone voice spilled out of the speakers.

"Yo, bro! How's it hangin'?"

Matthew chuckled, the familiar greeting reminding him of when they were just boys themselves. "High and steady," he responded, his head waving from side to side.

"Better than low and heavy," John answered with a deep laugh. "So, when do you take off?"

"I'm not. I signed up to mentor the kid who jacked my car and I need to put some things in place to do that. I'll postpone my trip until I can better arrange my schedule."

John laughed. "A personal, one-on-one butt whupping. Poor kid. Guess he didn't have a good lawyer."

"He had one of the best. That's why I'll be mentoring him and not someone else."

John nodded into the receiver. "You still need to take some time off. We all do. Fighting that hostile takeover drained our energy. The last few months have taken their toll on every one of us."

"So, why don't you and Marah sneak off to the islands for

a few days? The beach house is available. Your wife would like that, and since I'm staying, you won't have to worry about the office."

"Not much, anyway."

Matthew chuckled as he maneuvered his car through the throng of traffic that slowed his trip. "Not at all. I'll make sure no one burns the joint down before you return."

"I wasn't worried about *no one*. I was worried about you."

"Well, I won't burn it down, either. Nor will I give it away or send it into bankruptcy before the week is out. Next week, however, might be a different story, so you better take that time now and hurry on back."

His brother laughed. "Marah and I are on the plane as soon as I can get her packed. Thank you. I owe you one."

"Yes, you do," Matthew answered. "Send me a postcard."

"I'll do better than that. I'll bring you back some sand so you see what you missed."

"I love you, too," Matthew said with a wry grin plastered across his face. "Talk to you later!"

As he disconnected the call, Matthew guided his car toward the interstate leading to the ranch. He suddenly felt like riding his favorite black horse. It had been that kind of day.

"Why?"

Katrina took a deep breath, filling her lungs with warm air. Collin had just about pushed her last nerve and it was taking all her resolve not to explode. "Because I said so," she answered, her tone firm, the stern look she gave her son emphasizing that it was in his best interest to end their conversation.

"It's not fair!" the boy exclaimed instead, pouting profusely, as though he were five and not fifteen.

"Me spending my entire day in court over your nonsense wasn't fair, either, Collin. I had something else I would have liked to do, too. But you took that option away from me. There are consequences for our actions. You stole a car. You wrecked that car. You could have been injured. You could have injured someone else. Punishment for that is going to last you some time."

"But I'm being punished. The court is making me work for that man. It's not fair for you to punish me, too!"

Katrina chuckled. "You're lucky I don't go get me a switch from that tree out there. Then I'd show you just how unfair life is. Now, you are not going to the mall with your friends. You're not going today, and you won't be going tomorrow or anytime next week, so don't ask. In fact, if you don't go to your room and give me a moment of peace, you may not see your friends or the inside of a mall for another six years. Then you can tell me how unfair your sweet, spoiled life is. Do you really want to try me?"

She stood with both hands clutching the lean line of her waist. Her neatly arched eyebrows were raised high, her expression challenging. Collin heaved a deep sigh, then turned an about-face, muttering under his breath as he headed back up the staircase toward his room.

"And leave your phone on the table," Katrina called. "I told you no cell phone, no television, no nothing, and I meant it."

The boy paused. The look he tossed his mother was harsh as he came back down and dropped his new Droid onto the hall table. Minutes later, loud music echoed from upstairs, the boy's stereo turned up high. Calling his name, Katrina waited for a brief moment before silence filled the space.

She wasn't naive, though. She knew her son had only plugged headphones into the sound system. She'd give him until she herself climbed the stairs to her bedroom before she ordered him to turn it off, reminding him that "no nothing" included his beloved stereo system.

Moving into the kitchen, Katrina peered into the refrigerator for something to drink. It was way too early for her to

have a glass of wine, but she truly wanted a tall glass of char-
donnay. She hadn't eaten anything, though, and wine on an
empty stomach would not serve her well. She should have
stopped for lunch like she'd planned, but everything about
the morning's events had thrown her right off course.

She reached for a pack of pepperoni and some slices of
pepper jack cheese. Katrina mused that a light snack with that
wine would constitute lunch and that couldn't be so bad. She
popped a loaf of crusty French bread into her oven just before
uncorking the bottle and filling a crystal goblet with the elixir.
Savoring that first sip, she took another deep breath of air,
dropping down into a cushioned seat at her kitchen table.

If she were honest with herself, she would admit that dealing with her son hadn't been her greatest challenge that morning. She was accustomed to dealing with kids who'd made
mistakes, testing the limits of whatever authority ruled their
daily lives. She'd always known there would be moments with
her own child, although car theft had never crossed her mind.
She hadn't, however, imagined herself fighting the emotions
that a certain man had incited.

Matthew Stallion. Katrina took a gulp of her drink, a large
swig that was better reserved for shots of tequila, Jack Daniel's or a hearty beer, not the delicate wine that filled her glass.

The man's reputation had preceded him. In fact, because
of her own investment interests, Katrina had been closely following the recent events surrounding the failed attempt at a
hostile takeover of his family's business. Social Services and
the legal community had many good things to say about the
advocacy programs the Stallions had in place to assist families in need, especially the mentoring programs for students.
She'd been hopeful that she herself would be able to avail
herself of their services for some of the cases she knew she
would likely have to preside over in her new district.

Rising from her seat, she moved to the cherrywood cabi-
nets and pulled open a bottom drawer. Reaching beneath a

stack of papers, she lifted out a magazine hidden inside. The full-color image stared up at her, Matthew's seductive smile gracing the cover.

Texan Magazine had named the thirty-five-year-old man Bachelor of the Year, and he was looking every bit the part in the engaging head shot they'd captured. She imagined that he had garnered much attention from the honor. Katrina figured that a man like Matthew Stallion probably had no need for any help in that department, though, musing that he was clearly not a man who lacked female attention.

Reaching for her glass, Katrina took another sip, then remembered the bread, which was just a heartbeat away from being burned toast. Pulling the loaf from the oven, she dropped it on the countertop. She suddenly didn't have much of an appetite.

She sighed, blowing warm breath into the air. Katrina hadn't given any man a second thought since forever. The fact that she was giving Matthew a second, third and fourth thought completely unnerved her. But the man had been engaging. She'd been impressed with how he'd handled her son, seeming genuinely interested in the boy's well-being. Being someone that young men could look up to seemed foremost in Matthew Stallion's mind.

That enigmatic smile of his had caused her heart to race, her stomach to do flips as if she was on a roller-coaster ride. As they'd parted, he'd shaken her hand again, clasping it between both his palms, and the current of electricity that had rushed up her spine had left her breathless.

Katrina shook the memory from her mind, draining the last of her wine from the glass. *This is crazy,* she thought to herself, reaching to refill her glass. She was not interested in any man and particularly not in *that* man. Stuffing a slice of cheese into her mouth, Katrina shook her head from side to side. Convincing herself that she wasn't interested in Matthew Stallion was certainly proving to be the biggest challenge of her day.

Chapter 4

Matthew waited patiently on the stone steps of Greater Bethlehem Baptist Church. Sunday morning service would be starting at precisely eleven o'clock and he was excited that the Broomes family would be joining him.

Collin was scheduled to start his program that afternoon. When Matthew had called his mother to make the arrangements, he'd suggested they meet him for church first, then brunch, before journeying over to the ranch to give Collin the tour and explain what would be required of him over the next twelve months. Katrina Broomes had seemed reluctant at first, but with persistence Matthew had changed her mind.

Reflecting back on the conversation, Matthew couldn't help but note how reserved the good judge had been. Her cool demeanor had intrigued him.

"Church?"

Matthew had smiled into the receiver. "Yes, it's first Sunday, communion Sunday, but Pastor Barnes will have us out early. He's not one of those long-winded ministers."

"I don't know. I…"

"It will be good for Collin. I was raised in the church and it's done wonders for me," he'd said with a light chuckle.

There'd been a brief pause before she responded. "Collin's been to church before," she'd said with just a hint of attitude, as though he'd passed judgment on how she was raising her child. Then her tone had softened as she continued. "And it is good for him. I have to admit, though, that since we moved, I've been remiss in getting us up on Sunday mornings for service. I haven't found a new church home that we're both comfortable with yet."

"Well, I promise you'll both enjoy the experience. And afterward we can grab a bite to eat at Nicola's. They have a wonderful menu. So please, say yes."

Katrina paused, giving his offer some intense consideration. The man persisted.

"We could always eat somewhere else. Would you prefer French cuisine? I eat most anything, with the exception of fast food. I don't do burgers from any place that asks whether or not you want to supersize your meal."

Katrina laughed, her head waving easily from side to side. "What's wrong with their burgers?"

"Nothing, I'm sure. But a real meal involves real food. I know a great steak house, if you want something more traditional."

"Italian is fine. We'll meet you at the church," she finally responded.

Matthew's excitement spilled into the receiver. "Great. I'm looking forward to it," he said.

As he hung up the telephone, dropping the receiver back onto the hook, he suddenly felt awkward. He hoped the judge didn't think he was out of line. He'd been anxious, overly excited that she was amenable to his suggestions. He had really wanted to make their meeting a date but knew the timing would not be appropriate. He found himself hoping that she'd not found his behavior or his enthusiasm too inappropriate.

Shaking the memory, Matthew looked out to the parking lot just as Katrina pulled her BMW X5 SUV into an empty space. Matthew's smile widened into a full grin as he smoothed the front of his suit jacket, his excitement building.

As mother and son exited the car, Matthew couldn't miss the annoyed expression on young Collin's face nor Katrina's frustration as she admonished the boy to hurry up. Nor did he miss how stunning the woman was in her navy blue silk suit with its ruffled jacket. Even though the skirt stopped just above her kneecaps, there was no missing the long length of her toned legs and the curve of tight calves above her three-inch pumps.

Matthew had to remind himself where he was as he fought not to stare so blatantly. Mother and son climbed the stairs to meet him, Collin lagging noticeably behind.

Katrina extended her hand in greeting. "Mr. Stallion, I apologize. I hope you haven't been waiting long, but we were running a little behind this morning."

Matthew nodded. "Please, call me Matthew, and not to worry… I used to drag my feet and make my brother late every Sunday, too." He winked an eye in Collin's direction. "Mr. Broomes, it's a pleasure to see you again."

Collin eyed him warily. "Yeah, whatever."

Katrina shot her son a cautious glare. Matthew shook his head ever so slightly, his gaze meeting hers evenly.

"I've got this," he said softly, his hand tapping lightly against her arm. "He'll be fine." His voice rose ever so slightly, his tone deepening. "That will be the last time Collin greets anyone with disrespect." Matthew's gaze met Collin's directly. "Won't it be, Mr. Broomes?"

The look Matthew gave Collin made the boy take a step back, unsure what might be coming in his direction.

Matthew smiled brightly as he greeted Collin again.

"Good morning, Mr. Broomes. I'm glad you could make it this morning."

The boy nodded, his head bobbing ever so slightly against his lean neck. "Morning."

"It's Matthew, Mr. Stallion or sir. I know your mother taught you better. Try it again."

Collin paused briefly, looking from one face to the other as they stood staring at him. His mother appeared to be holding her breath, waiting for him to mouth off. His new mentor's stare was unreadable, the man's dark eyes only slightly menacing. He finally responded. "Good morning, Mr. Stallion."

Matthew nodded his approval. He directed his next comments to the two of them. "Why don't we go in and find a seat? My family is waiting for us."

Family? Katrina's eyes widened noticeably. The man had said nothing before about them joining any family. As he guided her into the sanctuary, her hand gently clutching the elbow he'd extended, she could feel her legs quivering ever so slightly. She tossed a quick look over her shoulder to see Collin following obediently behind them, his expression more curious than reproachful.

A uniformed usher led them to the front of the church, then guided them to what was clearly Matthew Stallion's usual seat. Katrina was only slightly taken aback by the two men who sat in the pews in front of and in back of them, both of whom bore a stark resemblance to the man by her side. They each possessed the same distinctive features: black-coffee complexion; chiseled jawline; dark, haunting eyes; plush pillows for lips and the same warm, welcoming smile.

Matthew paused to let Collin enter the pew first. Katrina followed, and he took the seat on the end.

He leaned over to whisper in her ear. "This is my brother Mark and his wife, Michelle," he said, patting the shoulder of the man in front of them. He gestured to the man sitting alone behind them. "And that's my baby brother, Luke."

Katrina smiled in greeting as both men wished her a good morning. A minute later John Stallion eased into the church, led by his wife, Marah. The brother named John gestured for Luke to slide down the pew so the two of them could take a seat beside him, tapping Matthew on the shoulder in greeting as he did. Marah leaned forward, her hand tapping Katrina lightly.

"Good morning," she whispered softly. "Welcome."

Katrina smiled again, words failing her as she sat there taking it all in. Morning worship service had yet to begin officially, but a praise session was in full swing. An elderly man was standing two pews in front of them, eulogizing everything he'd been blessed with since the last time he'd been in the sanctuary. He'd barely taken his seat before another senior citizen broke out in song. The atmosphere was warm and welcoming, and Katrina found herself tapping her foot to the music, pleased that she had made herself come. Even Collin seemed interested as he directed his attention to the students sitting in the choir stand.

Matthew had been right. The morning service went quickly. Holy Scripture was followed by prayer, the choir sang beautifully, and the pastor's message was short, sweet and to the point.

Standing beside her, Matthew was completely engaged. Katrina was moved by his devotion. As he bowed his head in thanksgiving, lifting his hands in praise, she sensed that he took that devotion seriously. Watching him, Katrina instinctively knew that Matthew Stallion was truly a man of faith.

As the pastor gave the benediction, Collin leaned into his mother's side, his head hovering just above hers. He dropped his chin down to her shoulder. Katrina smiled at him, her soft gaze meeting his.

"What did you think?" she asked him.

Collin shrugged. "I liked the music," he answered.

Matthew nodded his head in agreement. "That's my favorite part, too."

Behind them John laughed warmly. "I always thought the sermon was your favorite part," he said.

"Just like them passing the collection basket is yours," their baby brother, Luke, interjected.

The adults all laughed. Collin turned to stare at the men standing around him. His gaze came to a rest on Mark.

"Hey, I know you," he said suddenly, his large eyes widening with excitement. "You won the national bike race last year. You've won all the races."

Mark extended his hand, shaking the boy's heartily. "I'm Matthew's brother Mark. You must be Collin. We've heard a lot about you."

The boy grinned. "Hi!"

"And I'm Luke, and the old guy right there is our big brother, John," Luke said, introducing himself.

John nodded his head in greeting. "It's a pleasure to meet you both," he said as Matthew finished the formal introductions.

Marah smiled sweetly. "Judge Broomes, we'd love to have you join us back at the ranch for lunch."

Katrina smiled back. "Thank you, but..." She paused, tossing Matthew a questioning look.

Matthew interjected, "Thanks, Marah, but we have plans."

Marah nodded, clasping her arm around her husband's. "Well, if you'll excuse us, we need to say hello to the pastor before he disappears."

"It was nice to meet you both," Katrina said as the couple waved their goodbyes.

"We have to run, too," Mark said. He pressed a large hand to Michelle's blossoming belly. "Mitch and I are going shopping for baby furniture," he said, calling his wife by her childhood nickname.

Michelle rolled her eyes. "No, Mark's going shopping for baby furniture. He's just dragging me along."

"Congratulations. Is this your first baby?" Katrina questioned.

Mark nodded, his thick dreadlocks waving against his shoulders. "Yes, ma'am," he answered, leaning to kiss his wife's cheek. "My baby is having our first baby!"

Luke grinned. "This is quite an accomplishment for our brother."

Mark laughed. "You know it!"

Matthew chuckled. "What's on your agenda, Luke?" he asked.

"I'm spending the afternoon with Joanne and her parents."

"Where is your fiancée this morning?" Michelle asked, shifting her weight to one hip. "It's not like her to miss Sunday service."

"Her mother is here from Paris, and her father wanted them both to go to Sunday Mass at the Catholic church this morning. I thought I'd give them some family time together, so I passed. I told her I'd meet them afterward." The younger man took a quick glance at the diamond-encrusted Harry Winston watch on his wrist. "I need to get going, or I'm going to be late."

Luke winked an eye at Collin, who was staring at him. He punched his fist in Collin's direction and the young man met the gesture with a fist of his own, the two slapping palms and clutching fingers in the newest handshake. "Good luck, kid. He's really not so bad when you get to know him," Luke said, his eyes gesturing toward his brother.

Collin smiled. "Thanks, dude," he chimed, cutting a cautious eye at Matthew.

The family eased their way toward the front doors. The church's congregation had thinned out quickly. Matthew's fingertips lightly grazed Katrina's arm and back as he guided them forward. She felt a tremor of energy sweep through her.

Tossing a quick glance over her shoulder, she met his dark stare, saw the tender smile filling his face. The look he gave her was intoxicating, and she suddenly found herself consumed by the sweetest temptation.

"Is everything okay?" Matthew asked, his deep tone soothing.

Katrina nodded, a wave of nervous energy flooding the pit of her stomach. "Everything is fine," she answered softly, her gaze still locked with his. "Just fine."

But as she stepped out into the balmy afternoon air, butterflies dancing in her midsection, Katrina Broomes really wasn't quite sure of anything at all.

Chapter 5

Matthew had convinced Katrina to leave her vehicle in the church parking lot, assuring her it would be safe until they returned. Opening the passenger-side door of his Maybach Landaulet, he extended his hand to help her get in. When she was seated comfortably and was adjusting the seat belt around her petite frame, he nodded toward Collin.

"Once you're off probation and you get your driving permit, I might let you drive. Until then, though, you need to make yourself comfortable in the backseat."

"You'd let me drive this?" Collin asked tentatively. "Really?"

Matthew nodded, his hand braced against the rear door as Collin stood ready to step in.

"Yes, I would, but you'll have to prove that you can handle that kind of responsibility first." Matthew nodded again, gesturing with his head. "Now, hop on in. I don't know about you, but I'm hungry."

Minutes later they pulled into the parking lot of Nicola's Ristorante Italiano.

"This is very nice," Katrina said, taking in the surroundings.

As Matthew led them inside, she was impressed with the dramatic soaring ceilings, the elegant chandeliers and the rich, dark woods offset by splashes of crimson and gold. The atmosphere was sophisticated, intimate and a touch seductive. She was equally impressed with all the staff who greeted him by name, going out of their way to ensure that he and his guests were comfortable.

Matthew nodded as a hostess guided them to a corner table on the patio. "This is one of my favorite places to eat," he said. "The cuisine is northern Italian. All of the pastas are handmade. They don't have any freezers, so the groceries are delivered twice a day to ensure the ingredients are market fresh."

"We're very proud of our menu," the wide-eyed brunette waitress said as she placed glasses of ice water on the table in front of them. "Our chef is also an award-winning cook. And we have a wood-burning oven imported from Italy, too!" the woman exclaimed, her face beaming with pride.

Katrina smiled politely as the waitress turned an about-face and headed toward the kitchen with their orders. She could feel Matthew's eyes studying her intently, and she turned to meet his stare. Heat flushed his face, as if he'd been caught doing something he should not have been.

"Forgive me," he said, smiling shyly. "I didn't mean to stare."

Katrina blushed with him, cutting her eye at Collin, who was busying texting on his cell phone. She was a hair trigger away from reprimanding him but changed her mind, thinking the diversion would keep him focused on something other than her and this man.

"So," Katrina began, changing the subject. "Your family is very sweet. How many of you are there?"

"It's just the four of us—me, Mark, Luke and John. But we're steadily growing!" he said with a soft chuckle. "Wives and babies popping out all over the place! How about you? Any brothers or sisters?"

Katrina nodded. "I come from a *very* big family. I have three sisters and five brothers."

"There are nine of you?"

She nodded, amused by his expression. "Yep!"

"Wow! Were you all raised here in Dallas?"

She shook her head. "No. My mother was from Dallas, which is one reason I was drawn to the area, and my dad was born and raised in New Orleans. He's retired military, and we were raised on army bases all around the world. The family's in Arizona now, where my oldest brother settled down."

"My uncle Guy is an actor in California. And my uncle Mason owns a hotel," Collin interjected, never lifting his eyes from his cell phone.

Matthew smiled, nodding in the boy's direction. "And you only had one child?" he asked, turning his attention back to Katrina.

She smiled back. "Unfortunately I wasn't afforded an opportunity to have any more children."

Matthew sensed there was a story there and he wanted to ask more, but they were interrupted by their server and the platters of food being delivered to the table. He made a mental note to continue the conversation when they next had an opportunity.

An hour later Katrina could understand why the restaurant and its staff were so proud. The food was incredible. Matthew had taken the liberty of ordering for them and his choices had been right on point. Platters of hand-sliced prosciutto, Italian cheeses, fire-roasted vegetables, marinated olives, and fruit had started them off. Collin's eyes had widened with excitement at the presentation.

Tender veal chops topped with crispy pancetta and fontina

cheese and served on a bed of polenta with a white truffle infusion had been the main course for the two adults. Collin had opted for the homemade lasagna. By the time they'd finished their desserts of tiramisu, the ladyfingers soaked in just enough espresso and coffee liqueur, and traditional Sicilian cannoli, Katrina couldn't imagine being able to take another bite.

"Wow!" she exclaimed, leaning back against her seat. "That was incredible!"

Matthew smiled, a broad grin filling his face. "I'm glad you enjoyed it. Great food is one of my passions."

"Passions?" she replied.

Matthew's eyes widened suggestively as he leaned toward her. Unable to contain himself, he pressed his cheek to hers as he whispered in her ear. "Food can be very seductive. I'm very passionate about those things that whet *all* of my appetites." His tone was so low and seductive that Katrina found herself drawn to him.

Cutting her eyes at her son, who was eyeing them both curiously, Katrina felt a blush flood her face with color. Pulling her linen napkin to her lips, she met Matthew's gaze as he leaned back, clasping his hands atop the table. His expression was a penny shy of being smug. He winked an eye at her before turning his attention back to Collin, shifting the conversation.

Katrina felt as if a fire had been lit beneath her. The warmth of his breath against her ear, his cheek lightly teasing hers, had heated her from the center of her core outward. His husky tone had been enticing and suggestive. Had they been alone, she imagined that he would have ended the conversation quite differently, and definitely not so abruptly. She couldn't help but wonder where Matthew's insinuations might have led them if she'd been willing to follow.

Katrina suddenly imagined him slipping a hand beneath the table to caress her thigh. As if her body had a mind of its own, she felt her legs open at the prospect, imagining his large fingers teasing her flesh. His strong fingers tap-danced against her skin, heating her spirit until she was ready to implode from his touch. She gasped, pressing her legs tightly together as a tremor of heat spiraled between them.

"Mom!" Collin's anxious tone intruded on the decadent thoughts Katrina had been having about herself and that man. "I swear, you never listen to me!"

She shook her head from side to side. "Collin, please, don't raise your voice. I'm sitting right here."

The boy rolled his eyes skyward. "Boy, you were off in outer space! Mr. Stallion says that when I finish my chores at the ranch, then I can ride the horses. He says you can ride with me if you want. Isn't that cool?"

Katrina smiled, her gaze skating from her son's face to Matthew, who was staring at her intently. She nodded her head ever so slightly. "Yes, that's very cool."

"Do you ride?" Matthew questioned, his expression curious.

"It's been a while," she said with a slight nod of her head. "I've heard that you're quite the horseman, though. Is that true?"

His smile made deep dimples in his cheeks. "It's one of my many hobbies."

"Not a passion?" she said teasingly, surprised by her own boldness.

Matthew chuckled, his eyes twinkling with glee, as he leaned close one last time. "I hope you'll afford me the opportunity to share my passions with you, Katrina. I most certainly want to!"

His eyes shimmering with heat, Matthew rose from his seat, moving behind her to pull out her chair. As his fingers lightly brushed against her back, causing a shiver of heat to rush through her body, Katrina pretended not to notice the innuendo that eased like warm butter from his evocative tone.

* * *

The house was almost too quiet. Moving down the length of the hallway, Katrina stopped to peer into her son's room. Collin had fallen asleep with his clothes on, his lanky frame sprawled across the bedspread. His earbuds were plugged into his stereo, the sound system vibrating atop his nightstand.

She thought twice about waking him so that he could change into a pair of sleeping pants, but she didn't bother. It would only mean another fifteen minutes of her and him fussing at each other, and she'd had too good a day to end it on a sour note. Backing her way out of the room, she eased his bedroom door closed and headed back down the hallway toward her own room.

She'd had a great time with Matthew Stallion. From start to finish the day had gone better than she could have ever anticipated. The man had been thoroughly attentive to her, and to her child. He'd also been charming, funny and sexier than hell. She'd lost count of the times she'd imagined the two of them locked in a compromising position. She couldn't begin to fathom what in the world had gotten into her.

In the privacy of her bedroom she stood in front of the full-length mirror, staring at her reflection. She had always liked the woman who stared back at her. That woman was intelligent, articulate and dependable. There were some who thought her overly conservative and a tad stiff. There were only a select few in her inner circle who knew that she had a keen sense of humor and an adventurous spirit. And not since her late husband had she considered herself a sexual, sensual, desirable woman.

Katrina blew a deep sigh as she dropped down onto the side of her king-size bed. Kicking off her black pumps, she stretched her legs outward, twisting her ankles in small circles, her hands pressed tight against her upper thighs.

As she reflected back on her day with Matthew Stallion, she couldn't help but think that this might be as good a time as any for her to have a new beginning, something of a fresh start in her life. It would be only a few short years before Collin headed off on his own, and then she would have nothing else to do but think about herself. Would it hurt to start preparing early?

It had been aeons since she'd given any thought to her own needs and desires, every ounce of herself devoted to her son and her career. The prospect of a new relationship with a man who found her desirable was suddenly intriguing. Until that afternoon, having a partner, a companion, a lover and a new best friend all rolled up into one sexy chocolate treat had seemed as far from reality as·the complete obliteration of racism, sexism and every other ism that might exist. But Matthew had awakened an inner wanting that she had not allowed herself to have since forever.

A new beginning... Katrina couldn't refrain from imagining the possibilities. Lying back against the bed, she rolled over onto her side and pulled her knees to her chest, her body curling into a fetal position. Minutes later she was sound asleep, thoughts of her and that man spiraling through her dreams.

Chapter 6

The woman seated across the table from Matthew was chattering on and on as he sat nodding his head, fighting not to let his disinterest show on his face. He eyed the woman nonchalantly as he struggled to remember her name. It was Brenda or Linda or something like that, he thought to himself. He couldn't believe he'd actually forgotten the poor woman's name!

Matthew sighed, warm air blowing past his full lips, as she continued talking about nothing of any real importance. He might have managed to enjoy the date if he were able to think clearly, but after his day with Collin and Katrina, very little seemed clear anymore.

He closed his eyes for a split second, his head still waving up and down as he feigned interest. His focus, though, was elsewhere, his thoughts still lingering over the time he'd spent with Katrina and her son over the weekend.

Katrina had finally relaxed at brunch, seeming less tense as they'd eased into the comfortable setting and casual atmosphere. The conversation had been easy, calming any anxiety any of them might have been feeling. Collin had been disinterested, more concerned with the lasagna on his plate than anything else.

Matthew and Katrina had chatted easily, the exchange of conversation revolving around their respective careers and mutual interest in law and order. He had asked question after question, wanting to learn anything and everything he could about her. He was intrigued to discover that she had graduated from his alma mater, Harvard University, in Cambridge, Massachusetts. She'd been just as fascinated to learn that he'd walked the same hallowed halls just a few short years before her.

He'd been duly impressed to discover that she'd earned her undergraduate degree, her law degree, and had risen quickly through the judicial ranks to become a trial judge, while balancing the responsibilities of being a single parent. At the age of thirty-three she had much to be proud of. Her career had progressed quickly, her impressive legal acumen boosted not only by her acute intelligence but also her compassionate spirit. Her energy had shown in her eyes, her enthusiasm for what she did and how she did it clearly evident. Matthew had found himself hanging on to every word out of her mouth.

She'd referred to her late husband in passing. When Collin had jumped from his seat, rushing to the men's room at the mention of his father, Katrina had apologized profusely for his behavior. It was then that she told him she had married quite young, becoming a wife and mother before her nineteenth birthday.

"I don't regret any of it," she'd said softly. "Jackson and I grew up together. We'd loved each other since the third grade. At the time it only made sense for us to get married when we did. We graduated, went to the justice of the peace the very next morning, and nine months later Collin was born.

"Jackson went into the military so that we could both go

to school and take care of our son. I loved my husband very much and Collin is my life. But I definitely advise young women today to take their time before making such grown-up decisions. I had to make a lot of sacrifices to accomplish all that I have. Had I done things differently, it wouldn't have been half as hard. I was blessed to have my family's support the way I did."

Matthew nodded his head in understanding.

When Collin finally returned to the table, he attracted the interest of the young woman waitressing the table. She was especially attentive to their needs as she tried to engage him in conversation. Katrina shook her head from side to side, her eyes rolling skyward.

"These girls all think he's older than he is," she said as the waitress, a young woman named Brielle, rushed to bring them another order of baked bread.

Collin grinned. "Don't hate the player. Hate the game!" he gushed with a loud chuckle.

Katrina only shook her head with amusement. Matthew laughed warmly. When the young woman returned to refill their drink glasses, he couldn't keep from asking her a question.

"How old do you think he is?" he asked, his gaze moving from Collin to the young woman and back. He gave Collin a wide smile and Collin actually smiled back.

"Nineteen. Twenty, maybe."

Collin laughed, his excitement evident on his face. "Yeah, that's right!" he exclaimed, winking an eye at Matthew.

Katrina's head still waved from side to side. "No, that's wrong. He's only fifteen, and it'll be another ten months before he turns sixteen."

Brielle's eyes widened with shock. "Fifteen? You're barely in high school," she gushed.

Collin tossed his mother a look of annoyance before

answering. "I'm a freshman, but age is just a number. I'm a very mature fifteen-year-old."

Matthew laughed. "Very," he said teasingly. He turned to Brielle. "And how old are you?"

"Nineteen," she answered.

"Sounds like you two would make good friends someday," Matthew noted.

"Someday?" Collin repeated.

Brielle giggled. "Sure, young buddy. We can be friends!"

"So, I can call you?" Collin asked eagerly.

Brielle tossed Katrina a quick look before responding.

Collin's mother shrugged her shoulders, amusement still painting her expression. "He's allowed to talk to his friends on the telephone. When he's not on punishment, that is."

"Mom!"

The group laughed warmly. A smile hung on Matthew's face as he replayed each detail of their afternoon together over and over again in his mind. His name being called suddenly reminded him of where he was and who he was with.

"I'm sorry. What were you saying?" Matthew asked the woman seated opposite him. The Barbie-doll smile plastered on the anxious woman's face was hardly engaging, and Matthew couldn't help but note that she wore way too much makeup for his liking. He was suddenly having trouble remembering what it was that had attracted him to her in the first place, moving him to ask her out.

The woman with the bright smile leaned forward, resting her elbows on the table as she cupped her palms beneath her chin. She flipped her shoulder-length bob from side to side. "I was asking if something was the matter. You seem distracted this evening."

He smiled. "I apologize. I guess I'm a little tired. I've had a long day."

The woman reached a manicured hand out, the tips of her pink polished nails grazing his forearm. "We could always go to my place and *rest*," she said, the seductive overtones resonating in her soft voice.

Matthew chuckled. "Why do I get the feeling that *rest* would be the last thing we'd be getting?"

She stroked his arm back and forth. "Whatever are you thinking, Matthew Stallion?" she said coyly.

Matthew slid his arm out of her reach, easing it down to his side. "I'm thinking that we should call it a night. I've really enjoyed your company, but I am exhausted. I don't think I'd be much fun."

The woman persisted, leaning her body closer to his. "I can make it much fun for us both."

He smiled politely. "I'm sure you could, Tina, but tonight is really not a good night."

She huffed, rising abruptly from the table. "For the last time, my name is Leanne!"

As she stormed out of the restaurant, Matthew felt completely out of sorts. He hadn't meant to be rude, but truth be told, he hadn't wanted to be on that date in the first place. Had he followed his first instinct, he would have canceled. Had he been smart, he would have invited Katrina Broomes to dinner instead.

Settling back in his seat, Matthew inhaled, filling his lungs with air. He sent a quick text to his secretary with instructions to send the woman named Leanne a potted plant with an apology note first thing the next morning. A heavy sigh spilled past his lips. He couldn't believe how strongly he wanted to be with Katrina.

Her telephone ringing pulled Katrina from a light sleep. She glanced toward the digital clock on her nightstand. It wasn't quite ten o'clock at night. She had lain across her bed almost two hours earlier, intending only to close her eyes for a quick minute to catch her breath. Her day had started early, had been completely filled, and she'd been in need of a bit of rest before tackling a pile of legal briefs that rested on her desktop. She hadn't intended to fall asleep at all.

She pulled the telephone receiver to her ear, stalling the quick chime that was ringing through the room. "Hello?"

"Katrina, it's Matthew Stallion. I didn't wake you, did I?"

"Matthew! No, not at all," Katrina responded, the little white lie slipping out before she could catch it. "I was just settling down for the night."

"I didn't mean to interrupt. I just wanted to tell you how much I enjoyed our time together this weekend. I really had a good time with you and Collin."

She felt herself smiling into the telephone. It had been a good time. Their afternoon meal had been most entertaining, and the fun had continued back at Briscoe Ranch and the Stallion family's home.

Collin had been placed in the skilled hands of one of the youth-program counselors. The man had taken instruction from Matthew, his tasks for the boy outlined in full detail. For the first time that day her son had actually looked frightened. But Matthew had quickly eased his fears, and the counselor had swept the boy off to places unknown.

Matthew had escorted her to the family's rose gardens. They were a classic formal display of beds of roses arranged in a grass-girded oval around an exquisite marble fountain. Thousands of plantings and dozens of varieties decorated the landscape, and the sweet aroma wafting through the afternoon air was absolutely divine.

"This is beautiful!" Katrina had exclaimed, in awe of the scenery.

"Thank you. This is my sister-in-law's pet project. John's wife had the gardens installed shortly after they were married. It's a great place to sit and relax."

Matthew suddenly looked hesitant, pushing his hands deep into the pockets of his slacks. "Are you sure you don't mind my leaving you? As I explained when we talked, I really want

Collin to know that I am going to be directly involved with his curriculum."

Katrina had shook her head from side to side. "No, I don't mind at all. I brought a book to read, and I'm going to just sit back and enjoy the quiet."

Matthew smiled broadly. "What are you reading? A law review?"

A warm blush blessed her expression. "No, nothing quite that serious. It's a romance novel. I thought it would be a good diversion."

He chuckled. "A romance novel?"

Her right hand fell to her hip. "Something wrong with that?"

Matthew lifted both his hands up as if he were surrendering. "No, not at all. I'm sure I'd enjoy a good love story. Maybe you'll read one to me someday." His tone was suggestive; his eyebrows were raised questioningly.

Katrina simply shrugged her shoulders, the moment interrupted by the counselor ringing Matthew's cell phone to tell him they were ready. Politely excusing himself, he left her to her own devices, giving her ample opportunity to think naughty thoughts about the two of them.

Lifting herself upward in her bed, she heaved a deep sigh, shifting back into the moment. "We had a very nice time, as well," she answered softly. "Thank you for fitting us into your schedule. I know you're a very busy man."

"I was wondering…" Matthew began, pausing momentarily to gather his thoughts. "I was thinking that maybe you and I might have dinner together sometime this week. I would really like to spend some time getting to know you better."

Katrina paused. "I don't know if that's a good idea," she said, the hesitation rising in her tone. "I mean, with you mentoring Collin, and…" She stalled, her voice dropping off as she tried to collect her thoughts. "I don't know if it would be appropriate," she concluded.

Matthew chuckled softly. "I hardly think it would be inappropriate for two consenting adults to simply sit down and enjoy a meal together."

Katrina hesitated. For the life of her she wanted to come up with a hundred and one reasons why dinner with Matthew Stallion would be a bad idea, but she couldn't think of any plausible excuse to say no. It took her only a brief moment before she responded. "I'd love to have dinner with you. I'm free on Thursday," she said eagerly.

Matthew grinned into the telephone. "Great! I'll pick you up at seven."

"Matthew?"

"Yes, ma'am?"

"Thank you again for everything you're doing."

Matthew smiled into the receiver. "You're very welcome. Have a good night."

As she disengaged the call, Katrina's smile widened considerably. Her evening hadn't gone at all as she had planned, those legal briefs still waiting for her attention. But the high note that her night had ended on was simply the sweetest icing on some very good cake.

Chapter 7

Mark Stallion watched as Matthew paced from one end of the room to the other, glancing down at the watch on his wrist every few minutes. He grinned broadly and gestured with his head, meeting John's eye.

"Your brother's got it bad," he said.

John nodded, his own brilliant smile filling his dark face. "First time in a very long time."

Mark laughed. "Not since junior high school and that crush he had on Millie Stanfield."

John laughed with him. "I forgot all about him and Millie."

"I can hear you two," Matthew interjected. "And I did not have a crush on Millie Stanfield."

John swiped at the moisture that had risen on his eyelids. "I know that's right. You were head over heels in love until Millie slapped you in the back of the head for looking up her skirt."

Matthew rolled his eyes, stopping in his tracks to stare

down at the two men. "I would never have looked up Millie's skirt. I have always been a gentleman."

"You looked up her skirt, trying to figure out if her thighs were as thick as her calves," Mark teased.

Matthew shook his head. "That's not what I was looking for," he said with a sly grin. "But you boys wouldn't know anything about that."

"I know Millie slapped the fire out of you for sneaking a peek. She had your ears ringing for a month afterwards," John added, barely able to get his remark out in between laughter.

The three men chuckled warmly.

"So," John said, regaining his composure, "what's got you twisted tonight?"

"Don't you mean *who* has him twisted?" Mark questioned, his eyebrows raised.

John nodded. "And the answer to that would be…"

Matthew smiled, shrugging his broad shoulders skyward. "Spend half as much time minding your own business and you won't have any time to be minding mine."

John laughed. "Told you!" he said, gesturing with his head toward Mark.

Mark laughed with him. "I think he told you, too!"

"So, who's the lucky lady tonight?" John asked, his arms crossing over his broad chest.

Grinning, Matthew finally came to a halt, moving to take a seat in the leather wing chair that sat opposite his brother. "I'm having dinner with Katrina Broomes."

"Didn't you just have dinner with the judge?" John asked.

"We did brunch after church Sunday with her son. Tonight is an adult excursion. No one under the age of twenty-one permitted."

Mark nodded. "Sounds like you have plans!"

"I'm just going to make sure the woman has a nice time," Matthew responded.

John gestured toward the door and the driver who'd stepped

into the entrance to announce that he was ready whenever Mr. Stallion was. "I see you're taking the limo. I'm sure she's going to have a nice time, indeed."

Rising from where he'd briefly rested, Matthew moved toward the entrance. "Good night, John-boy. Good night, Mark. Don't you boys wait up for me. I'm sure I'm going to miss my curfew!"

The brothers chuckled heartily as they stared after their kin.

When Matthew was no longer in sight, Mark shook his head from side to side. "I've got twenty dollars that says he's dating a *Playboy* model by next week."

John shook his head. "You don't want to make that bet, little brother. I'm thinking Matthew might have finally met his match. I'd hate to have to take your twenty dollars from you like that!"

Katrina stood in the full-length mirror, assessing yet another outfit that might be fitting for her dinner date with Matthew Stallion. But it wasn't as if this was a *date* date, she thought, wanting to convince herself that the evening wouldn't be much of anything at all. It was, after all, just dinner.

She heaved a deep sigh at the navy blue suit that draped the wooden clothes hanger. It being just dinner didn't mean she had to go dressed like she was going to a business meeting, either, she mused. There had to be something in her closet that made her look more like a woman who might be in want of a man than a woman who was trying to compete with one.

Stepping into the oversize walk-in closet, Katrina scanned the multitude of dark blue and black garments that ran from one end of the space to the other. It took no time at all for her to determine that she really needed to upgrade her wardrobe. Nothing remotely feminine was hanging there for her to wear.

She heaved a deep sigh and reached for her cell phone,

punching in the speed-dial number to her best friend. After three rings, a woman's shrill voice called out her name.

"Katrina, why are you calling me? I thought you had a date?"

"What I have are dinner plans. It's not a date. And I'm calling you because I have nothing appropriate to wear."

Lacey Hamilton laughed into the receiver. "I'm sorry. You mean this isn't a suit-and-tie event?"

"Lacey, do you have a dress I can borrow, please?" Katrina asked, the exasperation ringing in her tone. "And I need it right now. My dinner companion will be here in thirty minutes."

Katrina could almost visualize the smug expression on her friend's face as the woman responded.

"Every time we go shopping, I keep telling you to expand your selections, but no, you're the one who keeps telling me that white blouses, granny skirts and black slacks will suffice. Now you want to borrow something a little sexier?"

"I never said sexy. I just don't want to look like I'm going to a business meeting."

Lacey laughed. "So who's the lucky guy?"

Katrina hesitated. "Matthew Stallion."

Lacey's tone perked up considerably. "*The* Matthew Stallion? Matthew Stallion of the prestigious Stallion family? *Legal eagle* Matthew Stallion? *That* Matthew Stallion?"

Katrina rolled her eyes skyward. "Yes. What does that matter?"

Her friend laughed warmly into the receiver. "I have just the thing for you," she responded. "Give me five minutes and I'll be right over."

Disconnecting the call, Katrina heaved a deep sigh and dropped down on the side of the bed. She trusted Lacey wouldn't disappoint her. The two women had been friends since they'd both prepared for the state's bar exam, studying together over iced cappuccinos and glazed doughnuts.

Katrina had purchased the home in gated Oaktree Estates based on Lacey's recommendations, the immaculate landscaping and the twenty-four-hour security detail. Her friend owning the house across the cul-de-sac from her had been a bonus. The woman was like a sister to her, and Katrina trusted her implicitly.

Fifteen minutes later Katrina stood staring in the mirror, suddenly questioning if her very best friend in the whole world had completely lost her mind. She didn't recognize the woman who stared back at her.

Lacey stood off to the side, her arms crossed over an ample bustline. Satisfaction painted her expression. "You look incredible," she said.

Katrina's wide eyes were glazed with shock. She shook her head from side to side. "I need to change!" she exclaimed, her voice quivering with emotion. "I can't go out like…"

Before she could finish her sentence, the doorbell sounded from the lower level. It felt like mere seconds before Matthew's deep voice resonated down below. He and Collin were chatting comfortably.

"You don't need to change," Lacey said excitedly. "You are going to take his breath away. You look fabulous," she added as she gripped Katrina by the shoulders and pushed her toward the door. "Now go have fun!"

Katrina was suddenly gripped with fear. What she was wearing was so uncharacteristic for her. Feeling completely out of control, she couldn't begin to imagine the evening going well at all. She should have worn the navy suit, she thought, blowing a deep sigh past her thin lips. But it was far too late for regrets, and she had no time at all to change into something else. Matthew Stallion was standing at the bottom of the stairs, staring up at her.

The muffled whispers on the stair landing above drew Matthew's eyes upward. Collin was leaning against the railing, his own gaze drawn to the movement at the top of the steps.

"Hey!" he exclaimed loudly, surprise painting his expression. "Is that you, Mom?"

Katrina rolled her eyes, ignoring him. Lacey bounded down the stairs in front of her, grinning broadly.

"Hi. I'm Lacey," she said, extending a hand in Matthew's direction. "Let's go, kiddo," she said to Collin. "You're hanging with me tonight."

"Do I have to?" the boy whined. "I'm old enough to stay here by myself!"

"Now! Let's move it," Lacey responded, tossing a quick glance back over her shoulder in Katrina's direction. Her hand was already on the front doorknob. "Make sure she has a good time," she said, directing her comment toward Matthew.

He nodded eagerly, his gaze still locked on the woman slowly descending the stairs. He was at a complete loss for words.

Stunning was hardly the word to describe the exquisite woman who was moving slowly in his direction. But Katrina Broomes was absolutely stunning. Gone was the conservative style that he had half expected. The dress that adorned her curvaceous frame was a formfitting cotton bouclé sheath with a sexy V back and an empire waist decorated with clear faceted jewels. The fabric stopped midthigh. Her lean, graceful dancer's legs were complemented by four-inch platform sandals.

Her hair cascaded in easy waves around her face and down about her shoulders. Her makeup was soft, complementing her angelic features. The woman was beautiful beyond words, and Matthew suddenly felt like she was a much-needed breath of fresh air. He inhaled her, drawing in a deep breath. It felt as if the sweet scent was nourishing his soul.

"Wow!" he exclaimed, the one and only word he could muster, though it was more an exaggerated gust of air blowing past his full lips. "I mean, wow!" he exclaimed a second time, his utterance feeling more substantial.

Katrina laughed nervously, a blush of heat tinting her cheeks. "Does that mean you approve?"

"Oh, yes, ma'am! I most certainly do!" His eyes were wide with appreciation.

"You clean up quite nicely yourself, Counselor," Katrina said teasingly. And he did. Right then, the man looked like a *GQ* model. She couldn't help but admire his black sports coat, gray slacks and white dress shirt, unbuttoned casually at the collar. A light tuft of black chest hair peeked from beneath his shirt, moving her to wonder what he might look like with his shirt off. Imagining him shirtless suddenly took her breath away.

Matthew felt like his face was on fire, heat flooding his dimpled cheeks. He couldn't remember the last time he'd been so excited about a woman. But Katrina had him excited beyond words. He blushed profusely, embarrassed at being so tongue-tied. He took a deep breath to calm his excitement, his broad smile widening. "Shall we go?" he asked, trying to keep his voice casual.

Katrina nodded, moving toward the door. As Matthew pressed a large hand against the small of her back, the two of them paused briefly, the heat sweeping between them suddenly consuming. Matthew met her gaze and held it; the lingering look she returned spoke volumes.

As they walked out the door, both cutting an eye toward the oversize mirror hanging in her front foyer, neither of them could miss just how attractive a couple they were together.

Chapter 8

"Was a limousine absolutely necessary?" Katrina questioned as they settled down against the leather seats.

Matthew nodded. "I didn't want to waste any of my time on anything but you tonight. If I don't have to drive, then you have my full and undivided attention." His smile was confident as he crossed an ankle over his knee. The comment moved Katrina to giggle ever so slightly, giggling not something she'd ever been known to do. Matthew's smile widened even more at the sweet sound of it.

"I should have asked if there was something special you wanted to do tonight," Matthew said sweetly.

"Dinner's good," Katrina responded with a slight shrug of her shoulders.

"You don't date much, do you?" Matthew said, the comment more a statement than a question.

"I make it a rule not to date at all," Katrina answered.

Matthew leaned toward her, using his index finger to brush a wayward hair from her face. He allowed his finger to linger lightly against her cheek. "Then thank you," he said softly. "I'm glad you found me worthy of breaking one of your rules."

Katrina found herself stammering for a response. "I… well…I…"

Matthew laughed. He reached for her hand and entwined his fingers with hers. "Relax. You don't need to be nervous. I just want you to have a good time tonight. Your friend put me on notice, remember?"

Shaking her head, Katrina laughed with him. She took a deep breath and then another. She couldn't help but note that her hand felt good locked beneath his. "I don't know why I'm so anxious," she said.

Sliding his body closer to hers, Matthew grinned. "I was hoping my devastating charm had you off-kilter."

Sliding across the seat to put some distance between them, Katrina smiled back, rolling her eyes skyward. "No," she said, her smug response moving him to laugh heartily.

He nodded. "I think you just told me a fib," he said teasingly.

She laughed with him. "You'd be right," she said.

With the ice broken, the two chatted comfortably and laughed easily as their vehicle glided toward the downtown area. Minutes later the limousine pulled up to the entrance of Cowboys Stadium and came to a stop. As the driver opened the door to let them out, Katrina stared in awe.

"Oh, my!" she exclaimed as she stepped out of the vehicle. Despite everything that had been written about the 1.3-billion-dollar building, it was like nothing she could have imagined. The enormity of its size made it seem as if an alien spaceship had landed smack-dab in the middle of Arlington, Texas.

Saying nothing, Matthew winked an eye as he wrapped an arm around her waist and guided her to the glass doors at the entrance.

The doe-eyed woman who met them there smiled in greeting, flipping a luxurious mane of bright red hair over her shoulders. "Good evening, ma'am. Mr. Stallion, sir. Welcome to Cowboys Stadium."

"Good evening, Melissa," Matthew answered, his head nodding ever so slightly. "Is everything ready for us?"

"Yes, sir. Everything you requested is in place. We're ready when you are, sir."

Katrina looked from one to the other, unable to decipher the cryptic conversation between them. Matthew winked at her again.

The woman named Melissa turned her attention toward Katrina. "Ma'am, may I take your wrap?"

Katrina shook her head, not quite certain that she was ready to let go of the lace shawl around her shoulders. It had become a protective shield of sorts, and she was clutching it tightly.

Melissa nodded, her bright smile beaming at the two of them. "Well, if there is anything else you're in need of tonight, please don't hesitate to let me know."

"I think we'd like to tour the facility before we dine. Unless, of course, you're hungry and ready to eat," Matthew said, turning his gaze to Katrina.

She shook her head. "No, a walk first will be fine," she said softly.

"Very good," Melissa said.

"Is there a game tonight?" Katrina questioned as they navigated their way through the main concourse and toward the elevators. "No, obviously not," she said, answering her own question, her voice echoing off the walls of the empty structure.

Matthew laughed. "No, we have the stadium all to ourselves tonight."

"The entire stadium?"

He nodded as he led her into the elevator and pushed

the button for the upper level. "Just us, the caterers and the woman with the key."

"And do you mind if I ask how you managed to pull that off?"

As the elevator came to a stop, the doors gliding open easily, Matthew paused. "I'm a Stallion," he said nonchalantly. The look he gave her was breathtaking, his self-assurance like a neon banner waving between them. She inhaled deeply as she pulled her right hand to her chest.

Entwining her fingers between his, Matthew guided her out of the elevator to the owner's lounge. He pointed to a large painting that decorated the wall.

"That's one of my favorite pieces," he said of the white-and-gray abstract. "The collection here is one of the most engaging exhibits in the state of Texas."

"Are you an art collector, Matthew?"

"I've acquired a few pieces. I like beautiful things," he answered. His gaze met hers and held it, the words feeling like a sweet caress against her ears.

Katrina blinked, shifting away from the emotion rising between them. "Everything is so massive," she noted as her gaze drifted from one work of art to another.

"That's how we do things here in Texas, ma'am," Matthew said, exaggerating his deep Southern drawl. "We breed everything big down here!"

She laughed, her head waving from side to side. "You are so *not* funny," she said as she rolled her eyes.

He pulled her hand to his lips and kissed the back of it. The sensation was electric, causing Katrina to gasp loudly. "That's why you laughed." Matthew grinned. "Are you ready for dinner, Judge Broomes?"

"Is that going to be big, too?"

Matthew took a step toward her, moving his body near to hers. Katrina felt herself holding her breath at the nearness of him. His fingers gently caressed the length of her arm as he spoke.

"I hope it will exceed your expectations," Matthew said, his gentle tone soothing. "I'm hoping this whole evening is going to be an event like nothing you've ever experienced before. If that takes big, then I assure you it will be the biggest meal you will ever have."

Easing her gaze up to meet his, Katrina suddenly wanted to kiss the full lips smiling down at her. The heat from his body had ignited a flame deep in her midsection, and she suddenly felt like she might combust from the intensity of it. She fought the sensation.

Her voice was barely a whisper when she responded. "I'd say you're off to a good start," she said softly.

Minutes later they were winding their way back through the main concourse, Matthew still pointing out the elaborate works of art that decorated the walls. The woman who'd greeted them earlier was waiting patiently in the immaculately decorated suite that led out onto the field.

"Enjoy your meal," she said as she gestured toward the fifty-yard line, where a dining table for two sat.

Katrina blinked in disbelief. Above their heads, a giant, center-hung video board, as big as two basketball courts, captured their entrance. Matthew was smiling smugly. She looked like a deer caught in headlights. Her eyes widened further when Matthew wrapped an arm around her waist and drew her close, leaning to press a damp kiss to her cheek. He laughed warmly, amused by the apprehension her expression held.

As they made their way across the field, Matthew pointed upward to the maze of stars that filled the evening sky. "I thought it would be nice to have them retract the roof so we could dine under the stars."

Her gaze lifted upward, Katrina stared in awe. "It's beautiful," she gushed. "Absolutely beautiful."

Matthew squeezed her fingers between his. "That's like the pot calling the kettle black, I think."

As they approached the center of the stadium, Katrina took in the immaculately set table. The dining table was adorned with an elegant white lace tablecloth, gold chargers, gold-trimmed china plates, gold utensils and crystal glasses. A tuxedoed waiter stood at attention.

Before she could respond to Matthew's "black kettle" comment, the waiter introduced himself, moving to pull out her chair.

"Good evening, madam, sir. My name is Jeffrey, and I'll be your waiter this evening."

"Thank you, Jeffrey," Matthew said.

"Good evening," Katrina chimed.

As they settled themselves in their seats, Jeffrey reached for a bottle of Moët & Chandon champagne chilling in a gold bucket filled with ice and water. He held it up for Matthew's approval. "Champagne, sir?"

Matthew nodded. "Thank you."

When both their glasses were filled, Jeffrey detailed their dinner menu. "For your pleasure tonight, we'll be serving all of the lady's favorites. We'll start your meal with melon and prosciutto in a spiced port wine reduction. Your second course will be braised beef short ribs with cheese grits and grilled squash. And for dessert, peanut butter pie with banana compote. If you're ready, sir, I'll be right back with your first course."

Matthew nodded his approval. "Thank you, Jeffrey." He turned his attention toward Katrina. "I hope you don't mind that I took the liberty of preordering our menu tonight."

Katrina shook her head in disbelief, her gaze following behind the man crossing the field. "All of my favorites? How did you know?"

"Your son. Collin also told me you have a thing for vanilla ice cream and chocolate syrup, but I understand that's reserved for days when you're ready to pull your hair out."

Katrina laughed. "I'll have to remind that child of mine that what happens at home is supposed to stay at home."

"Don't be too hard on the boy. He didn't know that I had ulterior motives for asking."

Katrina leaned back in her seat, folding her hands together in her lap. "Well, this is truly something, Mr. Stallion." Her gaze floated around the arena, taking it all in. "Is this how you typically wine and dine your dates?"

"I reserve moments like this for exceptionally special dates. And you're the first woman that I've had the pleasure of enjoying such a moment like this with, which makes you exceptionally special."

Katrina smiled sweetly, the bend of her mouth causing a ripple of energy to course through Matthew's midsection. As he smiled back, he couldn't help but sense that their evening together would be a great beginning to something very special between them.

"The entire Cowboys Stadium?" Lacey asked her excitedly. "For just the two of you?"

Katrina nodded her head as she dropped her weary body down onto her living-room sofa. The grandfather clock in the corner of the room ticked softly, the hands signaling that it was half past three o'clock in the morning.

"Yep!" She kicked off her shoes, twisting her ankles from side to side. "How was Collin? He didn't give you any problems, did he?"

Her friend shook her head no. "Collin was just fine. Don't change the subject. You actually had dinner on the field?"

"Smack-dab in the center of the fifty-yard line. We ate every last one of my favorites."

"That's amazing!" her friend said as she dropped down beside her. "Then what happened? What kept you two out until the wee hours of the morning?" she asked in a hushed whisper, her eyebrows raised suggestively.

Katrina laughed, her eyes rolling skyward. "Definitely not that! The man was a perfect gentleman. In fact, I barely got a kiss on the cheek when he brought me home."

"So what did you do for half the night?"

"We enjoyed dinner. Then we drove toward the aquarium and zoological gardens to a close-by café. We've spent the last five hours just talking. We'd probably still be there if I didn't have court first thing this morning."

"My, my, my! Y'all must have had some conversation!"

Katrina smiled, reflecting back on the entire evening. It had been some conversation between them. The two had talked about her, then about him. They found themselves laughing over mutual interests and pet peeves, discovering each other's idiosyncrasies. The man had moved her spirit, and when the night was done and finished, she found herself wanting to linger in the wealth of his energy. She couldn't remember the last time she'd enjoyed a man's company as much as she enjoyed Matthew's. Then she did, thoughts of her late husband slipping into her head. She inhaled swiftly, her eyes glazing over with tears.

"What?" Lacey asked, eyeing her friend curiously.

"I really like Matthew," Katrina said, meeting Lacey's inquisitive gaze. "I really like the man a lot."

Lacey chuckled warmly. "Don't sweat it. He likes you, too!"

"Do you think so?" Katrina asked, her tone suddenly anxious.

Her friend smiled. "You don't have doubts, do you? I mean, how could he *not* like you? How could any man that you are truly interested in *not* like *you?*"

Shaking her head, Katrina shrugged, her shoulders pushing toward the ceiling. "I'm not good at this, Lacey. This whole song and dance couples are supposed to do is so foreign to me. Trying to start a new relationship has me seriously traumatized."

"It's like riding a bike. Just get back on and pedal. The only difference here is that Matthew Stallion is like one of those elite racer bikes with all the gears and different speeds. That man has a lot of bells and whistles. You need to ride him right, or don't bother riding at all."

With a low chuckle, Katrina shifted forward in her seat. "That's exactly my point. Remembering how to pedal isn't my problem. But knowing when to shift might be a challenge. And not being able to figure out those bells and whistles is what I'm truly afraid of!"

Chapter 9

As Katrina changed from her judicial robe back into her linen blazer, she was glad that her day had finally come to an end. She had plans to meet Matthew for dinner and was excited by the prospect. He'd called early that morning, asking if she had any plans for the evening. Even if she had, she would have changed them without a second thought, wanting nothing more than to see the man one more time. She blew a deep sigh, her heartbeat racing at the mere thought of the man.

"Excuse me, Judge Broomes." The man at the door cleared his throat nervously as he sought out her attention.

"Yes, Mr. Jackson?" she said, turning to face the new clerk who'd been hired to assist her. The young man was fresh out of school, with a baby face, fire-engine-red hair and a pale complexion that would routinely transition from the palest pink to beet-red.

"There's a change in your schedule tomorrow. Both cases that were on the calendar have been postponed. It's too late to reschedule anything else, so you'll have the day off. That's, of course, if you'd like."

She nodded. "We actually have a ton of paperwork that I'd like to get through, so I will probably be here, anyway."

"Yes, ma'am. Will you be needing anything else this afternoon?" the young man queried.

"I don't think so, Mr. Jackson. I'm headed out the door, and I hope you are, as well. Anything special planned for this evening?" Katrina smiled warmly, easing her arms across her chest as she leaned back against the desk.

He smiled back. "No, ma'am. I just plan to relax with a good movie and a cold beer."

"That sounds like a plan to me. You have a good evening," she said, dismissing him.

"Thank you, Judge Broomes. Good night!"

As he turned and exited out the door, Katrina shook her head from side to side. Slowly but surely he was starting to relax around her. She was hopeful that the two of them would find a nice balance with each other to make their working relationship a pleasant one. Balance in her life was important to her, and since Matthew Stallion had her completely off-kilter, she desperately needed her professional relationships to be on point.

She took a deep breath, glancing down at the watch on her wrist. Matthew had promised her a quiet evening. She had asked him to define *quiet* so that they would both be on the same page. She instinctively knew by his teasing laugh that not only was he on a different page than she was, but they might actually be reading from two different books. She couldn't help but smile. Despite his assurances that she had nothing to worry about, she had to admit that she was a bit concerned.

Moving to the full-length mirror that hung on the back of the door in her office, she smoothed her hands over her charcoal-gray slacks. Although her white blouse contrasted nicely with the matching blazer, she couldn't help but think that her outfit needed a little spicing up. Once again her friend Lacey came through for her, this time without even realizing it.

Moving back to her desk, Katrina pulled a small bag from the bottom drawer. Dumping the contents of the bag onto the desktop, she smiled brightly. Lacey had gifted the contents to her months earlier, when she stopped by during Katrina's lunch hour after catching a sale at her favorite department store. The blue turquoise stones with their silver accents were the perfect adornment for her outfit.

She secured the clasp around her neck. The designer necklace sat comfortably against her collar. Moving back to the mirror as she secured first one and then the other earring in her ears, Katrina liked what she saw. As she stared at her reflection, she unbuttoned the top three buttons on her blouse. It was just enough to reveal a hint of cleavage. With a little cleavage showing, she looked less formal and definitely more feminine.

Inhaling deeply, she wished she could still the butterflies dancing in the pit of her stomach. But her excitement was building considerably as she thought about spending more time with Matthew. Taking a second deep breath and then a third, Katrina blew the warm air out past her thin lips. Satisfied with the reflection staring back at her, she reached for her leather handbag resting on the desk. Glancing at her wristwatch one last time, she headed out the door.

Katrina was doubled over with laughter, Matthew chortling heartily beside her. The two sat perched on bar stools in the Foundation Room lounge at the House of Blues. Both were wholeheartedly enjoying each other's company.

Matthew gave the bartender a quick wave of his hand, gesturing for the man's attention. "Bryson, my man, we'll both have another," he said as he pointed to the two empty shot glasses resting in front of them.

Katrina waved both hands in front of her. "No, no, no! No more for me," she said, giggling.

Her new best friend laughed with her. "Chicken!"

"I am not!" she said emphatically. "But you're a bad influence on me!"

"I beg your pardon!" Matthew exclaimed. "Your Honor, I'll have you know that I am the best thing that has ever happened to you. You just don't know it yet!"

There was a pregnant pause as the two sat staring at each other. Matthew's words vibrated against her eardrums, the truth of them settling comfortably over her spirit. His smile widened into a full grin. He pressed a heavy palm against her knee, gently caressing her flesh. Heat surged from his fingertips, igniting every nerve ending in Katrina's body. Her own smile widened considerably. She took a swift inhale, fighting to regulate her breathing.

"Thank you for dinner," she said finally, needing to move her focus as far from his touch as she could. "I've had a really great time."

Matthew nodded. "Me, too. But I hope you aren't planning to leave me just yet. It's still early yet."

She shook her head from side to side. "Not at all. I have a few hours till my curfew."

Matthew's grin was consuming. The moment was briefly interrupted as the bartender dropped two shots of Jack Daniel's down onto the counter. Matthew lifted both glasses, passing one to her.

"To us," he said, the simple toast implying much between them.

Katrina echoed his sentiments. "To us," she said as she pulled her drink to her lips and downed the bitter contents. She grimaced slightly, moving Matthew to laugh out loud again.

"We need to go for a walk," she said, pushing her shot glass away. "Before I'm not able to walk at all. How would that look?"

"That might be something for the record books," Matthew said teasingly. He dropped two twenty-dollar bills onto the counter and wished the man who'd served them good-night.

Reaching for her hand, Matthew entwined her fingers between his own. He pulled her along beside him, steering them out of the bar and restaurant. Outside, he looked up the sidewalk in one direction and then down the other.

"Where would you like to go?" he asked, focusing his gaze on Katrina's face.

She shrugged her shoulders. "I just want to walk," she answered, mindful of her left hand, which was still clasped tightly in his.

Side by side the two slowly made their way along the length of Laws Street, the view nothing more than a concrete parking lot. The quiet between them was comfortable, rising like a sweet mist and settling easily over their shoulders. Katrina crossed her right arm in front of her, resting her fingers easily in the crook of his elbow. She caressed the length of his forearm as she pressed her shoulder to his, leaning her body against him. The moment was enchanting.

Above them a full moon had risen in the night sky. The evening air had cooled nicely, and an easy breeze wafted gently about. The moment felt almost surreal, Katrina thought. As she contemplated what was happening between them, she was struck by a moment of doubt. Her growing emotions for the man were unexpected, and she admitted to being a tad bit scared. It wasn't her intent to express such thoughts out loud, but the effects of the Jack Daniel's seemed to have a different plan.

"I'm not interested in being a notch on your belt, Mr. Stallion," she said suddenly, the words spilling out of her mouth, as if they were on a mission of their own.

Matthew paused, reflecting briefly on her comment before responding. He squeezed her fingers gently. "Why would you say that?"

"Because I know about your reputation. I've heard what a notorious womanizer you are."

Matthew chuckled softly. "And you believe everything you hear?"

"I just don't want to get hurt. I couldn't handle falling in love with you, just to find out that I was only a number in your little black book," she said, the alcohol spilling the truth past her lips.

Matthew came to a standstill, turning his body to face her. He stared into her eyes, noting the saline that had glazed them. "And do you think you could fall in love with me, Katrina?"

Katrina met his intense stare. Her nerves were suddenly on edge, her knees quivering ever so slightly. "I…you…it's…" she stammered, suddenly at a loss for words.

Matthew eased his arm around her waist and pulled her to him, her body meeting his as if reconnecting with a long-lost friend. The connection was easy and comfortable, as if the two had been sharing moments like this since forever. Katrina pressed her palms to his chest, gently clutching the front of his shirt. Before she could rationalize what was happening, he glided his hand into her hair, his fingers teasing the nape of her neck.

When he lowered his lips to her lips, capturing her mouth beneath his own, whatever magic Matthew Stallion had performed on her, she was completely and totally under his spell. The kiss was like nothing she had ever experienced before. Energy seemed to surge between them, heat rising with a vengeance as his mouth skated with ease against hers.

When he pushed his tongue eagerly against her lips, moving her to open her mouth to him, Katrina moaned softly. He searched out her tongue, dancing a slow drag to a quiet beat that only the two of them could hear. The kiss was intense and consuming. Katrina felt as if she were being swallowed into a vast hole, floating through air on a cushion of intoxicating heat.

His lips were luscious pillows, and the man tasted like mint with a hint of Tennessee whiskey. The moment was perfection, every inch of him melding with her, as though the duo were two ideal halves coming together into a single unit. She suddenly couldn't imagine anything being sweeter.

As Matthew pulled her tighter to him, shifting his body even closer to hers, Katrina felt her whole body convulse from the pleasure. Needing to break the connection, she pushed him gently from her, gasping for air. Her gaze met his, his eyes wide with wonder.

"Was that a yes?" he whispered, his eyebrows raised.

Katrina's eyes flitted over his face, taking in every line and dimple, before settling on his eyes. "Don't tease me, Matthew. Please," she whispered back, her voice barely audible.

Matthew wrapped his arms tightly around her torso. He pressed his cheek against hers, caressing her soft flesh. Trailing a gentle path along her profile, he nuzzled his face against her neck, inhaling her perfume. The scent was one he recognized, Chanel No. 5, smelling like heaven against her skin.

"I'm not," he said softly. "I would never tease about something so important," he added as he tucked a hand beneath her chin and lifted her face to his. He dropped his forehead to hers, a deep sigh easing past his full lips.

"What's happening with us?" she questioned, the words a soft whisper against his ears.

Matthew's gentle smile lifted to a coy grin. He smiled sweetly. "This," he began, his mouth brushing warmth against her earlobe. "This is sheer magic."

Closing her eyes tightly, Katrina savored the enchantment of the moment. Matthew still held her tightly, the heat from his body teasing every one of her sensibilities. She found herself wishing that the two of them could stay that way forever. Matthew's seductive voice brought her back to the moment.

"You still haven't answered my question. Katrina Broomes, do you think you could fall in love with me?"

Opening her eyes, Katrina met his intense stare. The answer was perched precariously on the tip of her tongue, ready to spring out with no regard for the potential consequences. Her heart was beating her response in a rhythmic syncopation that could easily rival a marching band's drum line.

Reclaiming some sense of self-control, Katrina simply shrugged her shoulders, her response shimmering in her dark brown eyes. And then she kissed him again, throwing every doubt and concern to the wind.

Chapter 10

Matthew should have been expecting the woman sitting in the leather executive's chair behind his desk. Her frequent visits were as regular as clockwork, but each time he walked into his office to find Vanessa Long ensconced in his seat as if the space were hers and not his, it surprised him. As he swept into the room, depositing his briefcase on the desktop, Vanessa was pouting profusely, seemingly annoyed at something across his computer screen.

"Hey," she said, not bothering to raise her eyes to see who might be standing before her.

"Good morning, Vanessa. Get out of my seat, please." Matthew said, his bemused tone moving her to lift her gaze to stare. The pause between them was only momentary. "I said please." Matthew smiled, gesturing with his index finger for her to get up and out of the way.

"Is that how you speak to the mother of your unborn child?" she asked, leaning back in the chair and clasping her fingers together over her very pregnant belly. Her smile was smug.

Matthew's eyebrows lifted, his amusement draining swiftly from his face. "Don't play like that, Vanessa. That is not funny. I don't need to tell you that I am *not* that baby's father."

Vanessa laughed warmly, her smug smile twisting into a coy grin. "We both know that, playa, but everybody else isn't so sure. I think it's fun to keep them guessing."

"I think you better find some other way to amuse yourself. Now get out of my chair," he said as he clasped her gently under her arm and helped her to her feet.

Rolling her eyes in mock exasperation, Vanessa moved to the other side of the room and dropped her heavy body down on the leather office sofa. She heaved a deep sigh, one eye clenched shut, as the tightness in her abdomen rolled from one side to the other.

"Junior thinks you're a riot," she said as she gasped for air, a swift kick to her insides knocking her breath away. "Ouch! I swear, when this kid gets here, there is going to be some major payback for all he's putting me through!"

Settled in his own chair, Matthew studied her closely. Vanessa Long had been a part of their family since elementary school. Best friends with his brother Mark, Vanessa and the Stallion clan had grown up together. For as long as Matthew could remember, Vanessa had been all tomboy, her daredevil antics rivaling those of most males. For a brief moment, she and Mark had been boyfriend and girlfriend, the rest of the family thinking the two would end up head over heels in love with each other. College changed the dynamics of their relationship, as it was then that Vanessa admitted her predilection for women. Each of the Stallion men had only been slightly disturbed when their family friend finally came out about her sexuality. And over time they had all found their balance, Vanessa acting as if she were just one of the boys and Matthew and his brothers treating her so.

Then, one year ago, Vanessa had approached Matthew for a favor, swearing him to secrecy. Vanessa had wanted to be a mother, anxious to experience that side of being female. With Matthew's assistance Vanessa had sought out the best sperm bank in the nation. After they decided on a clinic that was widely recognized in the health-care industry for the quality of its donors, its use of molecular genetics testing for infectious diseases and its chromosome analysis standards, he had helped her navigate all the legal ramifications of selecting an anonymous donor and buying sperm.

Despite the depth of friendship she shared with his brother Mark, she had asked Matthew to hold her hand at her gynecologist's office during the insemination. Afterward, the two had shared a plate of sushi and Vanessa's dreams for a child that would be half her and half donor number 0004169, a man purported to speak five languages and to have the muscular, athletic build of a quarterback, an acute sense of humor and a love for arts, music and sports.

Matthew had only been mildly surprised when she chose him, and not Mark, to help her. He respected her for not wanting to intrude on her best friend and his wife, Michelle, as the two navigated the joys of their own pregnancy. He was, however, completely shocked by the number of family members and friends who thought not only that he might have actually fathered Vanessa's baby himself, but also that he would be reluctant to take responsibility or acknowledge his paternity. Having handled all Vanessa's legal obligations, Matthew was bound by the attorney-client privilege to remain silent, so he'd allowed them all to think what they wanted, neither denying nor confirming anything.

He watched as Vanessa struggled to get comfortable, her bloated body causing her much angst. Pregnancy had blown the tiny woman up considerably, making her look like some type of wobbling toy with a too-tiny head and toothpick legs.

As he watched her roll from one side to the other, Matthew chuckled softly.

"So, what did I do to deserve the pleasure of your company this morning?" he asked.

"I had some papers to drop off to the ethics department before I met your brother's wife for some baby shopping."

"What are you and Mitch after today?" he asked curiously, referring to his brother Mark's wife.

"Breast pumps," Vanessa said, clutching both of her melon-size breasts in the palms of her hands and jiggling them. "Mitch's idea, not mine."

Matthew laughed. "That still doesn't explain why you came to see me."

"I figured there was no point in wasting a prime opportunity to stir up some office gossip about the two of us. Give the kids something to mull over during their lunch hour." She laughed heartily as she continued, "Is he or isn't he the father of her baby? It's the million-dollar question, you know."

"With the two-dollar answer. Matthew, you are *not* the father!" Matthew said mockingly.

Vanessa laughed again, and then, just as quickly, the exuberance in her eyes was replaced with a wave of sadness as she fell into deep reflection. Matthew continued to eye her curiously.

"What's wrong, Vanessa?"

She shook her head from side to side, shrugging her shoulders to the ceiling. "I'm thinking that this might not have been a great idea. What do I do when Junior wants to know about his father? What do I tell him?"

Matthew was silent, the enormity of her question provoking some thought. He rose from his seat, moving to her side. Taking the seat beside her, he wrapped a thick arm around her shoulders.

"I think it might be a little late to be having doubts, Vanessa, don't you?"

The woman blew a deep sigh. "Your bedside manner sucks," she said, elbowing him lightly. She swiped at her eyes with the back of her hand.

Matthew laughed. "Your hormones are impacting how you're rationalizing things right now. We've been through this before. When the time is right, you will tell your child the truth. You will tell him how much you love him and how much you wanted him. Then you will tell him that the method you chose to conceive him was the best option for you at the time. You will tell him what you do know about his father and apologize for his father not being in his life. Then you'll send him over to the ranch for me, Mark, Luke and John to do the rest."

Vanessa leaned her head against his shoulder. "You sure you don't want to be my baby's daddy?"

Matthew laughed. "I'm positive. I'm also sure that I need you to stop making jokes about it. Seriously, it might get me into trouble."

Vanessa turned to stare, something in Matthew's tone drawing her attention. "And you're suddenly worried about that, Mr. Stallion?"

Matthew became silent because he was worried about it. More than he'd realized. With the relationship growing between him and Katrina, he couldn't afford for anything about himself to be misconstrued.

Katrina. A wave of something unfamiliar wafted through his midsection, the sensation causing a shiver of energy to race down his spine. He felt himself shudder in response.

Could she fall in love with him? The night before he'd pressed her for an answer, but she'd ignored his appeals. Her body language, however, had spoken volumes, the kiss between them like no kiss he'd ever shared before. Holding her in his arms, he hadn't wanted to let go, intent on holding tight to her for as long as he possibly could. He'd wanted an answer, though, needing to know if what seemed to be happening to him was happening to her, as well.

Blowing a sigh, he shook the fragments of memory from his mind. He felt Vanessa studying him intensely, and he lifted his gaze to meet hers. He could only imagine what his friend was trying to decipher from his behavior. But what he did know was that he didn't need Vanessa bird-dogging him for answers that he himself didn't even have yet. And he also knew that Vanessa snooping into his personal life would be like having the FBI, the CIA and Homeland Security all searching for gold at Cartiers. Nothing would be sacred; no stone left unturned.

He dropped his hand against Vanessa's blossomed belly. The life inside kicked his palm, seeming to acknowledge his concerns. He smiled.

"I just don't want there to be any misunderstandings about our relationship," he said finally. "I respect your privacy, obviously. But I also hope you'll respect my not wanting this to impact my personal life any more than it already has."

Vanessa was still eyeing him curiously. "What's her name?"

Matthew laughed, ignoring her question. He looked down at the diamond-encrusted watch on his wrist. "Don't you have someplace you need to be?"

She laughed with him. "You know I'll find out, so you might as well tell me. Give me all the juicy details."

Matthew came to his feet. "Goodbye, Vanessa. I do have work to do."

"Well, I'll be John Brown!" she exclaimed excitedly. "You really are serious about someone! She must be something special."

Matthew moved back behind his desk and paused. He met Vanessa's anxious gaze and held it for a brief moment before responding. "Yes, she is exceptionally special," he said, a wide grin filling his dark face. "More than you know. And that's all I'm going to say on the subject, so leave it alone."

Vanessa smiled broadly, approval washing over her expression. "Good for you, big daddy! Good for you!" She moved toward the door, her hand on the doorknob as she paused. "And thank you," she said, tossing him a quick glance over her shoulder.

"For what?"

"For being such a good friend."

Matthew smiled with her, noting the familiar hint of mischief in the woman's bright eyes. "I mean it, Vanessa. Sweet-talk me all you want, but stay out of my personal life!"

After tossing him a quick wink, Vanessa gave him a wave of her hand. When she was outside the closed door, Matthew could still hear her laughing heartily.

Katrina shifted the pile of papers in front of her, rearranging the documents with ease. "And how does the defendant plead?" she asked, lifting her eyes to meet the stare of the defense attorney before her.

"Guilty, Your Honor. This is Mr. Briggs's first offense, and due to the nature of his crime and his age, he qualifies for the Extended Day Youthful Offenders Program at the Clemens Unit."

Katrina nodded, shifting her gaze toward the state prosecutor, who stood across the aisle from the other attorney. "Is that correct, Attorney Daye?"

"Yes, ma'am."

"Now, enlighten Mr. Briggs and myself for a moment. The program encompasses what exactly?" she questioned.

The district attorney nodded. "It's a sixteen-hour daytime program at the state's youthful offender institutions, designed to provide at least twelve hours of activities. The program is structured to include work assignments, vocational and academic instruction, counseling, behavior modification, military-style drills, systematic discipline and other opportunities that will reduce inmate idleness and enhance the young inmate's chance at becoming a law-abiding citizen upon re-entry into the community."

Katrina moved her gaze to the young man standing at his attorney's side. "Mr. Briggs, did your attorney explain this clearly to you and did you understand it?"

The lanky redhead with the freckled complexion nodded, twisting his hands nervously in front of him. "Yes, ma'am."

"And you understand that even with a plea of guilty, this court is under no obligation to accept the plea bargain offered to you by the state?"

"Yes, ma'am," the Briggs kid said, cutting a quick look at his defense attorney.

"All right, then, the court accepts the plea of guilty. Mr. Briggs, per the proposed plea bargain agreement this court remands you to the Clemens Unit youth facility for a duration of six months. With good behavior and upon successful completion of the program, you will serve an additional six months of house arrest, followed by one year of state-monitored probation.

"Mr. Briggs, this court hopes that you will utilize this time wisely. You're being offered an opportunity to change your life around, so please make the most of it. And if I ever see you in my courtroom again, you can trust, sir, that I won't be so lenient."

Katrina slapped her gavel against the wooden desk as an officer of the court took the young man into custody. Behind him, his family was nodding their support, heads bobbing up and down, as tears streamed down his mother's face.

"This court will recess until one o'clock for lunch," she said, rising from her seat.

"All rise!" the court bailiff cried out, motioning for everyone in the courtroom to stand up.

As Katrina closed the door to her private chamber behind

her, she blew a soft sigh. Cases like this one taxed her energy. She'd heard five cases in total that morning, each one involving students under the age of nineteen. Their crimes ranged from petty misdemeanors to vicious felonies.

Dropping down onto the leather chair behind her desk, she extended her legs out in front of her, twisting her ankles from side to side. On top of the desk, a lunch bag waited for her attention, her assistant having bought her a salad and a sandwich minutes earlier.

But food was the last thing Katrina had on her mind. Matthew Stallion had her attention, and thoughts of the man had her head spinning. Closing her eyes, Katrina allowed the memory of their time together to sweep through her spirit.

Matthew Stallion was definitely a man she could fall in love with. Katrina had no doubts that she wasn't the first woman to have thought so. Everything about the man had her enamored. He was charming, compassionate, spirited and just too damn sexy for words. There was something about being in his arms that made her lose perspective, made her unable to focus on anything but the two of them together.

Katrina suddenly found herself longing for the heat of his body. There was something in his touch that just felt good and right, burning deep into the core of her spirit. And his kisses…what she wouldn't give right then and there to feel him kissing her like he'd kissed her the night before.

Shaking her head from side to side, Katrina couldn't believe this was happening to her. She was falling in love. Matthew Stallion had her so wide-open that she couldn't begin to imagine herself going back to a life without him in it. She found herself shaking as the reality of the fact settled around her.

A knock at the door pulled her from her reverie. Drawing herself up in her seat, she shook her thoughts of the man out of her head, then called for the person on the other side of the door to come inside.

Chapter 11

Collin stared at his mother, his expression a combination of concern and annoyance. Katrina had been humming softly since she'd pulled the car out of the garage, maneuvering in the direction of the high school. He couldn't remember the last time he'd seen his mother so oblivious to her surroundings and not uptight about something.

"Do you have money for lunch?" Katrina suddenly asked.

Collin shook his head. "No, ma'am."

"Get a twenty-dollar bill out of my purse."

"Twenty dollars?"

"Won't you need a few dollars for after school?"

Collin looked confused. "After school?"

"For a snack. I saw some vending machines in the recreation room at the ranch."

"Oh," Collin said as he pulled the money from his mother's wallet. "What's gotten into you?" he asked curiously.

Katrina looked in her rearview mirror and then her side

mirror before tossing her son a quick glance. "What do you mean?"

"You've been really weird lately," he said as he twisted his twenty dollars between his fingers. "Like superweird."

Katrina laughed. "Just because I'm in a good mood, I'm acting weird?"

Collin shrugged. "It's just not normal."

His mother nodded her head slowly. "I need to ask you something. It's very important." She paused, taking a deep breath. "You know I went to dinner with Mr. Stallion the other night?"

"Yeah."

"How do you feel about that?"

The young man shrugged his shoulders, pushing them skyward. "It's okay, I guess. Why?"

Katrina paused again, her eyes skating back and forth as she contemplated what she thought she needed to say. "Well, you know that Mr. Stallion and I have become really good friends. I wanted to know what you thought about that."

Collin rolled his eyes. "You two aren't dating, are you? Come on, Mom. You're too old to date!"

"Thanks a lot. I didn't realize I was that ancient."

"That's not what I mean. It's just not…" The boy paused. "It's just weird."

Katrina nodded. "Yeah, it is a little strange." She tossed him a quick smile before turning her eyes back to the road. "But I think it's something we will both have to get accustomed to."

Collin shook his head from side to side. *You might have to get accustomed to it,* he thought to himself. *I don't have to get accustomed to anything.* He cut an eye toward his mother, noting the goofy smile that painted her expression. He scowled, his face twisting with annoyance.

Matthew Stallion was okay, but Collin wasn't interested in any man moving into their lives permanently. He had only a few months to go before he finished his court-ordered sentence, and then he and his mother could go back to things being the way they were before she met that guy. Collin wasn't much interested in having a token father around. But until he could figure out a way to make sure Matthew Stallion went on his merry way, he'd make the most of the situation.

His eyes suddenly widened with excitement. "Hey, since you're in such a good mood, can I go to the water park with Tyler and Nick and 'dem during break next week?"

"And who is chaperoning this excursion?"

"Nick's brother. He's twenty years old."

Katrina laughed, cutting her eyes at her son. "Uh, no!"

"But everyone else is going!"

"Does everyone else have a parent going, too?"

"I thought you were in a good mood?"

Katrina laughed. "A good mood does not mean I've lost my mind and gone stupid. Therefore, no parents and no adult supervision means no trip to the water park."

She pulled her car into the high school's driveway, joining a lengthy line of buses and cars dropping off students. Collin persisted as he waited for an opportunity to jump out of the car and join his friends.

"Can I at least go to the mall this weekend? Please?" he begged. "I promise I won't get into any trouble."

Katrina smiled, hesitating for a quick minute. Her son's anxious gaze met hers. She was suddenly taken aback by the maturity of his features, the facial hair sprouting above his lip and across his chin. The boyish lines that had been so acute just weeks before were gone, and he had suddenly matured, becoming the spitting image of his father. As if a bolt of lightning had struck her spirit, she was suddenly gripped by the reality that her baby boy was truly no longer a baby.

Pulling into an empty parking space, Katrina heaved a deep sigh. Her thoughts were interrupted by her son's anxious tone.

"So, can I?"

"We'll see how the rest of the week goes. Stay on track, do everything you're supposed to do, and then ask me again on Saturday. Deal?"

Collin grinned, his hand on the door handle. "Cool!" he exclaimed excitedly, swinging the door open. "See you later."

Katrina called after her son.

"Yes, ma'am?"

"Do you think you could give your mother a kiss good-bye?"

The young man rolled his eyes skyward, glancing over his shoulders to see if any of his friends were looking. Leaning back across the seat, he pressed his lips to his mother's cheek as Katrina wrapped her arms around his torso.

"I love you," she said softly, pressing her palm to his cheek.

"Yeah, yeah, yeah," Collin replied, pulling back from the embrace. He grinned as he made his way out of the vehicle. Then he leaned back inside, his smile widening even further, mischief shimmering in his wide eyes. "I love you, too, Mom!" he exclaimed, before turning an about-face and racing after the boys who were waiting for him at the entrance to the school.

Pulling out of the school's parking lot, Katrina adjusted the Bluetooth earpiece in her ear. She'd already programmed Matthew's cell-phone number into her phone directory, and after a quick push of a button she waited as the phone rang on the other end, both her hands gripping the steering wheel with anticipation. When Matthew answered the call, she was grinning widely.

"Good morning, gorgeous," Matthew purred. "You must have been reading my mind, because I was just about to call you."

"Good morning to you," Katrina responded, her voice dropping to a seductive lilt. "I hope I'm not interrupting anything."

"No, not at all. I was just sitting here in my office, missing you. Wondering what you were up to this beautiful morning."

"Actually, I just dropped Collin off at school and now I'm headed to court."

"How's my buddy doing?"

"He seems to be making a genuine effort to get himself back on track. But you know how that goes. I'm just going to take it one day at a time."

Matthew nodded into the receiver. "So, when do I get to see you again?" he asked anxiously.

Katrina's grin was illuminating. "I was hoping you might be free for lunch, actually. I only have one case on the docket this morning, and then I'm free for the remainder of the day. Do you have plans?"

"I do now," Matthew said. "Do you want me to pick you up?"

"I'm not sure exactly what time we'll be finished, so why don't I just come get you at your office when I'm done?"

Yes, Matthew thought to himself as he tossed his head back, pumping his fist in the air in a gesture of accomplishment. He answered her in a calm, even tone. "That sounds like a plan. I'll see you soon, darling." Disconnecting the call, he did a little happy dance behind his desk, shuffling his feet in excitement.

Lost in her own exhilaration, Katrina sat in complete awe of the familiarity that seemed to have bonded them together. Distracted, she completely forgot that she was stopped at a stop sign, until the driver of the vehicle behind her blew his horn to get her attention. With a wave of apology she looked left and then right before proceeding through the intersection and continuing on her way, thinking that her morning had truly started out nicely.

There were two women in deep conversation when Katrina stepped off the elevator on the twentieth floor of the Stallion Enterprises Building. The woman seated behind the desk was gently patting the other woman's very pregnant belly, and the two were cracking jokes about stretch marks and swollen nipples. When Katrina stepped up to the desk, both women paused in surprise.

"Good afternoon. I'm here to see Matthew Stallion. My name is Katrina Broomes."

Carol, Matthew's secretary, nodded and smiled sweetly. "Good afternoon, Judge. Please, go right on in. Mr. Stallion is expecting you."

Nodding, Katrina returned the bright smile. She met the other woman's curious gaze. "Congratulations. When are you due?"

Vanessa Long smiled back. "About ten more weeks. Less, if I'm lucky!"

"That's very exciting. My baby is fifteen now. It's the best thing that will ever happen to you and your husband," Katrina said.

Vanessa nodded, cutting her eye at Carol. "I'm very excited," she said, not bothering to mention that she had neither a husband nor a baby daddy to speak of.

Katrina gave Vanessa a warm smile as she moved to the office door, her hand dropping to the doorknob. "Good luck!" she exclaimed. With one last look over her shoulder, she pushed open the door and stepped inside.

As the door closed behind Katrina, Vanessa directed her stare at the other woman. "So, you think she's the one?"

Carol nodded, her eyebrows raised. "I hear they've been spending quite a lot of time together."

Vanessa nodded with her, the wheels beginning to spin in her head. "Very interesting," she muttered under her breath. "Very interesting indeed."

Behind the closed door Matthew Stallion looked up, his face brightening with excitement. Katrina's wide smile greeted him warmly.

"Hey, you!" he exclaimed, rising from his seat and moving quickly to her side. He wrapped her in a warm embrace, planting a moist kiss against her cheek. "I didn't think you were ever going to get here."

"I apologize. Court ran longer than I anticipated. I hope you're still hungry."

Matthew waved his head up and down. "Starved," he said as he nuzzled his face into the curve of her neck, trailing a line of kisses across her jawline.

Katrina giggled softly, a current of heat surging deep in her abdomen. She pressed both her palms against his broad shoulders, savoring the sensation of his touch. When Matthew moved to press his lips to hers, the passion in his kiss made her knees quiver, and her legs threatened to drop her to the carpeted floor. It was only his arms wrapped tightly around her waist that kept her standing tall.

When he finally pulled away, Katrina was completely lost in the moment, her eyes shut tightly, her body quivering with the want of more. It was Matthew's hand, gently drawing a slow caress along her profile, that moved her to breathe again, enabling her to let go of the breath that she had been holding so tightly.

"Mmm, mmm, mmm," Katrina muttered softly, finally opening her eyes to stare into his.

Matthew chuckled, the warmth of his laugh searing her spirit. "You can have more of that once you feed me."

"Promise?"

"Cross my heart!" he exclaimed excitedly. "So, where would you like to go for lunch? 'Cause I'm hungry."

Katrina's smile was electrifying as she grinned back at him. "Actually, I've made plans for us already. I hope you don't mind."

"Not at all. I like it when a woman takes charge."

"Then you should be a very happy man, because I like having control."

Matthew laughed heartily. "I just bet you do, woman! I just bet you do."

* * *

Outside it had begun to rain. In the backseat of her SUV Katrina and Matthew were cuddled close, his arms wrapped warmly around her torso as she sat between his opened legs, leaning back against his chest. Matthew's back was supported by the leather seat and the window. His right leg was extended across the leather upholstery, and his left foot was resting on the car's floor. Both had abandoned their shoes to places unknown. Matthew's suit jacket and tie were tossed across the front seat. The front windows were cracked open ever so slightly, a damp breeze blowing about the space.

Matthew took a deep inhale of air and then two more, filling his lungs with the fresh, earthy scent of the outside. The air was warm and teasing. Katrina felt the up-and-down rise of his chest against her back. She snuggled down closer to him, pulling his right arm tighter around her torso.

The afternoon had sped by, time seeming to kick into high gear the minute the two of them had stepped out of the Stallion corporate offices into the afternoon air. Since then the two had been talking for hours, their depth of sharing moving to a whole other level. Matthew found himself feeling slightly vulnerable as he opened up to Katrina, allowing her to hear his fears and insecurities, things he'd never shared with anyone, not even his brothers.

Katrina, too, felt more exposed than she'd ever felt before. But she also felt secure, completely confident that whatever she shared with Matthew would remain between them. His demeanor was protective and nurturing, warming every ounce of her spirit. She was acutely aware that she was trusting him with her heart and hoped that he could sense that his own was safe and shielded deep in the pith of her soul.

"This is probably the best picnic I've ever had," he said, his warm breath blowing against her neck and ear.

She laughed softly, nodding her head in agreement, despite

her best-laid plans having been blown completely out of the water by the mild storm that had buffeted the town.

The rain had started to fall even before they stepped out of the vehicle, which was parked on the perimeter of the Jonsson Color Garden at the Dallas Arboretum. The blanket she'd brought for them to sit on outside was still folded up and was now resting somewhere on the floor of the luxury vehicle. It had been her idea for them to crawl into the backseat to dine on the meal of French Brie, crusty bread, roast chicken and fresh fruit. The bottle of dry rosé that she had chilled at home in her fridge had been kept cold in a small cooler with ice packs.

Matthew offered her the last of the bottle's contents before tilting it to his own full lips, emptying it in one swallow.

"I have had a great time, too," Katrina said, her voice coming in a loud whisper. "I hate that it has to end."

"It doesn't," Matthew whispered back. "Not if you don't want it to." He drew the backs of his fingers down the length of her arm to her hand, entwining her fingers with his.

"You're a smooth talker, Mr. Stallion. I can see why women lose their minds around you."

Matthew laughed warmly. "Have you lost your mind, Ms. Broomes?" he asked as he pressed his lips to the back of her neck, his tongue drawing a damp path on her skin. The surprise of it caused Katrina to jump ever so slightly, heat rushing through her feminine spirit. A slight throbbing erupted between her legs, and her nipples suddenly pressed hard against the silk lining of her brassiere. The sweet ache had her wanting to come right out of all her clothes.

Needing to put some distance between them before she did something completely foolish, Katrina shifted around in the seat, moving her body to sit upright. Matthew's smile was smug as he slid his leg from behind her and sat upright himself.

"Are you okay?" he asked.

"It's getting a little warm in here," she said, fanning her hand in front of her. "Very warm."

Matthew pressed his shoulder to hers. "I hadn't noticed," he said, shifting his leg until their thighs were touching.

"Right!" Katrina exclaimed, still fanning herself.

Matthew met her gaze, his stare intense as his eyes washed over her face, focusing on the soft curves of her mouth. Her slight smile was consuming as her lips parted ever so slightly. When she pushed her soft pink tongue past the line of her pearl-white teeth to lick her lips moist, he found himself completely enamored.

Without any thought he wrapped his arms back around her body and pulled her to him, dropping his mouth to hers. He kissed her with complete abandon, wanting to lose himself in his want of her. When Katrina kissed him back, wrapping her arms around his neck, he felt himself harden in his slacks, his manhood rearing up for attention. Matthew wanted her, the proof of that wanting undeniable. Desire had surged full force, and it took every ounce of constraint for him to maintain control.

Matthew leaned back, pulling Katrina down on top of him. The kiss intensified as he slowly licked her lips with his tongue, easing his way inside her mouth. Reaching for the back of her throat, his tongue danced in sync with hers. Both of them were breathing heavily when Katrina suddenly became aware of his hands dancing under her blouse, his fingers kneading the flesh along her sides and back. When his thumb eased beneath her bra strap, and Katrina felt that the garment might suddenly snap free, she stiffened ever so slightly.

She suddenly couldn't believe that she was making out in the back of a parked car as if she was a teenager, no thought being given to her prominent position in the judicial system or to the fact that the man she was with was a much-idolized member of the Dallas community. She couldn't believe that they'd both completely lost their minds.

Extricating herself from his embrace, Katrina gasped for air, a blush of color flooding her warm complexion. Matthew's body quivered, a current of electricity igniting every nerve in his body. Perspiration had beaded across his brow.

"Okay," he muttered with a deep chuckle. "Maybe it is getting a little warm back here."

Katrina laughed, not missing the evidence of his discomfort as Matthew pushed open the car door, stepping out into the mist of rain. He stamped one foot and then the other, trying not to draw attention to his need to adjust himself in his pants. Sliding across the leather seat, Katrina stepped out behind him, the blacktop wet against her bare feet. She hesitated briefly, clutching the back of his white shirt before wrapping her arms around his waist and leaning her body against his. She pressed her cheek against his upper back and inhaled the scent of him.

Matthew caressed the backs of her hands, her fingers locked together across the tight line of his abdomen. His breathing had eased; the light mist of rain had slowly cooled his body temperature. Turning an about-face, he wrapped her deep in the wealth of his thick arms and hugged her gently, pressing a kiss to her forehead. The realization that he had fallen head over heels in love with her was suddenly overpowering. The words were on the tip of his tongue, but he didn't say them out loud, still surprised by how "I love you" sounded in his head.

Chapter 12

After a very long day, Matthew slowly made the drive to the magnificent Preston Hollow estate on Audubon Avenue. The man couldn't get Katrina off his mind. He couldn't remember any woman ever having his full and complete attention, and Katrina Broomes clearly had his. He marveled at the woman's accomplishments and her dedication to her profession and her family. She was clearly a force to be reckoned with, and he found her straightforward demeanor and conservative edge to be quite sexy. He loved that she didn't mince words, shooting straight from the hip. She was a woman who didn't play games, and she made it clear where she stood on everything.

And he wanted her. He wanted her like he had never wanted any woman before. Whenever they were together, he wanted to touch her. The nearness of her ignited a flood of emotions deep within him, and all he could think about was wrapping his arms around her and holding her close to him. He relished the heat from her body mixing with his own. It nourished his spirit, and in those moments in her company he felt full and complete. The desire was consuming, and he wanted to taste her, imagining himself drawing his tongue against the sweetness of her skin. Every single thought he had about the woman aroused him. He wanted her, and more importantly, he was almost desperate for her to want him, too.

The honorable judge was a woman after his own heart, and the more Matthew thought about her, allowing his mind's eye to reflect back on all their time together, the more he found himself contemplating her having his heart, and everything else he possessed. He banished the sensation from his thoughts, his head shaking from side to side as he tried to pull himself together.

Easing his vehicle through the gated entrance to the grand home, he pulled into an empty parking spot and shifted his car into Park, shutting down the engine. His mind was still racing, every nerve ending in his body feeling as if it was ready to implode. Heaving a deep sigh, he exited the car and took in his surroundings, stopping to stare at the front of the house.

Constructed of Austin stone with copper accents and a tile roof, the European-style residence easily encompassed some fifteen thousand square feet of living space. It sat on some sizable acreage, the expanse of landscaping boasting a putting green, an Olympic-size swimming pool and tennis courts. It was the first home John had purchased for the brothers. Now only Mark and his wife, and their baby brother, Luke, resided there. Although Matthew hadn't lived there for some time, he'd suddenly felt a need to return to their family home.

Making his way to the iron-and-glass entrance, Matthew dug deep into his pocket for his keys. Closing and locking the door behind him, he tiptoed across the marbled foyer and into a handsome study that was complemented by Brazilian cherrywood floors, wall-to-wall bookcases and a beamed ceiling. Inside, his brother Mark was seated in a leather wingback chair, a glass of umber-colored drink in his hand. A single light burned dimly from the desktop.

"Hey, what brings you here tonight?" Mark asked, eyeing him curiously.

Matthew shrugged, reaching for the decanter of brandy and his own crystal goblet. "Didn't feel like going to my apartment tonight. What are you doing up?"

Mark heaved a deep sigh. "Couldn't sleep and I didn't want to wake Mitch. My baby needs her rest."

"How's she doing?" Matthew asked, concern shining in his eyes. "The pregnancy is going okay, right?"

"The doctor says she and the baby are both doing just fine. Mitch is nervous, though. It won't be too much longer now."

"And how are you doing, Dad? You scared?"

Mark met his big brother's stare. He shrugged his broad shoulders. "It's crazy, Matthew. I don't think twice about taking a suicide curve, doing over one hundred miles per hour on a quarter inch of bike tire. But the mere thought of holding an eight-pound infant scares the crap out of me. I don't want Mitch to know I'm scared, but I'm scared!"

Matthew laughed. "I'm sure once that baby is here, it'll be a piece of cake. You're going to make a great father. Just remember everything John ever taught us, and you'll be just fine."

Mark nodded, taking a slow sip of his drink. He paused momentarily before changing the subject. "Mitch and I had dinner with Vanessa tonight." He cut his eye in Matthew's direction.

Matthew cut his eye back. "And how is Vanessa doing?"

"Like Mitch. She's ready for it to be over and the baby to be here."

Matthew nodded. He blew a deep sigh as he took a large swig of his drink.

Mark laughed. "She told us about what she did…the insemination, I mean. I swear, I don't know about that woman sometimes! You know, I had twenty dollars bet on you being the father."

Matthew shook his head from side to side. "You should have known better."

"That's what John said."

"Does he know, too?"

Mark nodded. "She told the whole family, but she asked us not to tell anyone else."

"Well, that's a start," Matthew said, a slow smile pulling at his mouth. He nodded, dropping deep into thought.

The two men sat in silence for some time, both reflecting on their personal lives and the new life that was about to change everything they all knew. Matthew shifted awkwardly in his seat.

"What's eating at you tonight?" Mark asked, sensing his brother's anxiety.

Reaching for the decanter, Matthew filled his goblet a second time. He took another swig, blowing a heavy sigh after he swallowed. He didn't have words to explain what was happening with him. It was like something had gotten under his skin and was growing steadily, threatening to consume him. He wanted to shake the sensation of Katrina from his head, but thoughts of the woman refused to let him go. And he wasn't ready to expose the truth of that to his brother, wanting to keep his desire for the woman to himself so it didn't become fodder for the family to take bets on, as well.

"I'm just tired. I'm sure after a good night's rest, I'll be just fine," he said, rising from his seat.

"I hope so," Mark said, a smug expression crossing his face. "Now that Vanessa's let you off the hook, you need to be on your toes if you're going to make things work with the judge. I hear she's one tough cookie."

Matthew turned to stare in Mark's direction, his eyebrows raised. "I swear! Is nothing sacred in this family?" he questioned.

His brother chortled heartily. "You really didn't think Vanessa came clean because she had nothing better to do, did you? She just didn't want us looking at you funny, since you and the judge are officially a couple. At least that's the story Vanessa is telling, and she says the odds are in her favor that she's got this one right. About you and the judge being official, that is."

"And let me guess, you took a bet that Vanessa is wrong?"

Mark laughed. "Not this time, big brother. I learned my lesson after I had to pay John twenty bucks the last time I bet on you."

The two brothers laughed warmly. Making his way out of the room, Matthew wished his sibling a good-night.

Mark called after him. "Hey!"

"Yes?"

Mark lifted his glass in a mock toast. "It's all good, man. It's all good. It has happened to the best of us. Falling in love is a beautiful thing, family. It's a beautiful thing!"

It was well past midnight but Katrina couldn't sleep. And she couldn't stop thinking about Matthew. She couldn't stop herself from wishing he were there with her, resting beside her for the night. She imagined that if she could curl herself against the hard lines of his body, she could easily fall asleep in his arms. She wanted to fall asleep in his arms. She heaved a deep sigh.

Rolling onto her back, she tossed her arms over her head, kicking the covers from around her feet. She was in awe of the relationship she and Matthew had managed to build. Months earlier had she even imagined the possibility of being so happy with any man, she would have readily dismissed the thought from her mind. And here she was now, happier than it should ever be possible, an unlikely blessing coming when she least expected it.

The past few months with Matthew Stallion in her life had

opened a whole other world to her. One she'd thought was lost forever to her when her late husband was killed in action. She had suddenly found that she had not only a best friend and a confidant but also a partner who wanted his future to be about the two of them together, his dreams interlocked with her own.

Lately they'd been talking about taking their relationship to another level, both of them yearning to take their union in a more intimate direction. Katrina was finding it more and more difficult to hold back, to contain the desire that rose with a vengeance each and every time they were alone together. Matthew had even confessed his own difficulty with leaving her with just a kiss at the door after their many dates together. The wanting was beginning to take on a life of its own.

Katrina sat upright in her bed, pulling her knees to her chest. She was acutely aware of the many women who would have already given up their goodies to the handsome man, not thinking twice about spreading themselves open for his pleasure. It wasn't that she was purposely holding out, but that no time or place ever seemed right. With thoughts of their jobs, their positions in the community, and her child seeming to always intrude on the moment, Katrina had just not allowed herself to take that step.

She also knew that it was her own hesitancy that held Matthew back, the man seeming to sense that she wasn't quite ready to step over that threshold. Not once had he ever asked why or pressured her for more than she'd been willing to give.

But she was ready. More than he realized. It was knowing that once they did that deed, there would be no turning back that had her totally afraid. Katrina knew that when that happened, Matthew would own her heart, her soul *and* her body, and she needed reassurance that he would want all of her for the rest of their lives. She needed that reassurance because she knew, given how she was feeling now, that making sweet love to Matthew Stallion would have her never wanting to let the beautiful black man go.

Chapter 13

Briscoe Ranch had well over eight hundred acres of cattle pastures and an equestrian center. Back in the day, Edward Briscoe, the ranch's original owner, had been one of the original black cowboys. Not long after the birth of his three daughters, Eden and the twins, Marla and Marah, he'd expanded his Texas longhorn operation. He and his first wife had added an entertainment complex that specialized in corporate and private client services. The ranch now housed two twenty-thousand-square-foot event barns and a country bed-and-breakfast.

After Marah Briscoe's marriage to John Stallion, Edward had signed the property over to his daughter and new son-in-law, and so it came to fall under the Stallion Enterprises umbrella. With the property being central to Austin, Houston, Dallas and Fort Worth, Briscoe Ranch had made quite a name for itself. It had also become a second home to all the Stallion men, the dynamics of the close-knit family drawing them even closer together.

As Matthew made his way up the front steps for the requisite monthly family breakfast, the sound of laughter from the rear of the large country home spilled out onto the front porch. The joy of it made him smile. Moving inside, he sauntered through the foyer, calling out a rousing hello as he entered the large family room and kitchen.

His brothers, John, Mark and Luke, returned the greeting, tossing up their hands in hello from where they sat at the oversize table. At the stove and kitchen counters, the women—John's wife, Marah; her sisters, Eden and Marla; Luke's fiancée, Joanne Lake; Mark's wife, Michelle; and Juanita Briscoe, Edward's second wife and the Stallion boys' surrogate mother—were busy prepping the morning meal. Juanita moved toward Matthew, dusting her hands against a kitchen towel before reaching to press her cheek to his face. She kissed him warmly.

"Good morning, baby!"

"Good morning, Aunt Juanita. How are you doing today?"

Juanita nodded her head, twisting her hands together in front of her. "I'm doing well, Matthew. How are you doing?"

"Exceptionally well."

"I hear a good woman will do that to a man," Edward Briscoe said, moving into the room behind him. He clapped his palm against Matthew's broad back.

The Briscoe sisters all raised their eyebrows, curious.

Marah chimed in warmly, "Is that right, Matthew? Has a good woman done that to you?"

"A good woman we might know?" Eden asked.

The men gathered around the table laughed heartily.

"You might as well spill it," Luke said, leaning back in his seat as he crossed his arms over his chest. "If you don't, you know we'll all make up our own versions of what's going on."

"Or believe what Vanessa is telling us," Mark added.

Matthew shook his head from side to side, laughter brimming past his full lips. "Mr. Edward, what is it you always say? If we spent six months minding our own business, and six months staying out of everybody else's business, we wouldn't have any time to poke our noses where they don't belong. Is that right?"

His brother's father-in-law laughed heartily. "I think what Matthew is trying to tell all y'all is that you need to be out of his business."

Matthew winked an eye. "Thank you, sir. I appreciate that translation."

Juanita sucked her teeth, rolling her eyes. "I swear, if all you boys don't stick together like flies on stink!"

Edward leaned forward to give his wife a quick squeeze. "Learnt it from you womenfolk!"

Everyone in the room laughed.

Mark echoed the sentiment. "I know that's right!"

"You don't know any such thing at all," Michelle said as she eased her very pregnant belly over to take a seat beside her husband.

Mark cut an eye in John's direction, meeting his brother's gaze as the man chuckled softly. Both men knew not to say anything in response, Michelle and Marah both eyeing them keenly.

Moving to his usual seat, Matthew laughed as he sat down. "When there is something to tell, I promise, you all will be the first to know."

"I doubt that," Luke said, nodding his head as Vanessa suddenly bounded into the room. "Not if the mouth of the South has anything to say about it."

They all laughed as the youngest brother gestured in Vanessa's direction.

"Good morning, everybody!" Vanessa chimed.

They all responded in sync. "Good morning! Hey, Vanessa!"

Vanessa plopped down onto a cushioned seat. "How's everyone doing this morning?"

The men all nodded. Matthew met Vanessa's gaze, and she raised her eyebrows, a sneaking grin spreading across her face.

"What's up, big daddy?" she asked, humor painting her tone.

Matthew shook his head from side to side. "Not much, Vanessa. How are you doing this morning?"

"Ready to bust! Junior's kicking up a storm this morning."

From his seat at the head of the table, Edward leaned forward in her direction. "Miss Vanessa, what's up with calling that baby Junior? You know that baby a boy, or you just guessing?"

Vanessa shrugged her shoulders. "I really don't have a clue, Mr. Edward. Junior could be a boy or a girl. I want to be surprised."

"Oh, you're gonna be surprised, all right!" Edward exclaimed, his head waving from side to side. "Puts me in mind of a joke I know," he said.

His daughters all rolled their eyes skyward. Marah groaned out loud.

"Daddy!" Eden exclaimed.

"Tell your joke, Mr. Edward," John interjected. "Don't pay these women an ounce of attention!"

Edward chuckled, his gray head bobbing against his thin neck. "A police officer saw a man dressed as a cowboy in the street, complete with a huge Stetson hat, spurs and his six-shooters. 'Excuse me, sir,' said the police officer. 'Who are you?' 'My name's Tex, Officer,' said the cowboy. 'Are you from Texas?' asked the police officer. 'No, sir,' said the cowboy. 'I'm from Louisiana.' 'Louisiana?' said the police officer. 'So, why are you called Tex?' The cowboy said, 'I wouldn't want to be called Louise, would I?'"

John cut his eye at his wife as he laughed.

Marah shook her head. "That was so not funny, Daddy!" she said.

Her sisters nodded their agreement.

The patriarch flicked his hand at them in annoyance and then turned his attention to Mark and Michelle. "What about y'all? Do you two know whether or not yo' baby is a boy or a girl?"

Mark grinned, cutting his eye at his wife. "Maybe we do.... Maybe we don't."

Michelle rolled her eyes. "Yes, sir, we do know."

Everyone in the room was silent, their gazes moving from one to the other.

"Well?" Luke finally said. "Are you going to tell us or what?"

Mark laughed. He looked at his wife. "I don't know. Should we?"

Michelle smiled. "You play too much," she said to her husband. "You know you're dying to tell them, so I don't know what you're waiting for."

Juanita walked up behind Mark and gently slapped the back of his head with her hand.

"Love tap!" the Stallion men all chimed in unison, laughing heartily.

"Stop fooling around," Juanita said as she placed a platter of freshly fried bacon on the table.

Mark was still grinning as he winced ever so slightly. "Ouch, Aunt Juanita. That wasn't nice."

"It's not nice of you to be keeping us in the dark. We all want to go do some baby shopping, so tell us something."

Mark clasped Michelle's hand beneath his own. "Mitch and I found out this week that we are having…" He paused, looking around the table as everyone sat with bated breath.

"A baby girl," Michelle interjected, rolling her eyes at her husband a second time. "And we plan to name her Irene. Irene Stallion, after your mom." A blanket of silence fell over the room as she looked from one brother to another.

Mark met John's gaze. John stared for a brief second, then

smiled, his head nodding against his thick neck. John rose from his seat and moved to Mark's side. The two men clasped hands and bumped shoulders, clinging tightly to each other. Luke and Matthew rose to join them, and the four men hugged each other warmly.

"Mom would have liked that," John said softly. "She would have liked that a lot."

Mark swiped at the moisture that had risen to his eyes.

The rest of the family stared, each of them fighting back their own tears. The moment was more emotional than any of them had anticipated.

Matthew and Mark punched fists, Matthew nodding his approval, before they all moved back to their seats. Matthew fell into deep thought, suddenly wishing that Katrina was there by his side to share in the moment. He looked up to find Vanessa staring at him as she slowly rubbed her pregnant belly. She smiled sweetly, seeming to sense his thoughts, her gaze wishing him all the very best the future might have to offer. Nodding his head ever so slightly, he smiled back, knowing that Vanessa knew he wished only the very best for her, as well.

Clearing her throat, Vanessa interrupted the moment. "I'm sorry," she said as she pointed to her swollen stomach, "but Miss Irene's new best friend is starving and something smells really good."

Everyone laughed out loud.

Lifting platters of food from where they rested, Joanne and Marla moved the freshly cooked food from the counters and stove to the center of the dining table. Each of the family members took their usual seat, all of them making room where room might be needed. The conversation moved from babies to food, the passing of platters becoming everyone's focus.

"Blueberry muffins!" Luke exclaimed excitedly as Joanne

placed two on his plate. He leaned over to kiss his girl's lips. "You must have been reading my mind!"

Joanne giggled ever so softly. "Not hard to do, baby, with you wishing you had some blueberry muffins every day for the last week."

"Doesn't hurt to toss out a hint or two every now and then," Luke responded. He bit into a moist muffin, savoring the taste of vanilla and blueberry against his tongue.

"Or nine or ten, knowing you," Matthew interjected.

"So, have you two set a wedding date yet?" Juanita asked.

Joanne and Luke both cut their eye at the other. Luke shrugged his shoulders as Joanne began to hum.

"Well…um…we…um…" she began.

John laughed heartily. "We'll take that as a no."

"We're enjoying ourselves," Luke said, reaching to hold Joanne's hand beneath his own. "We know that we're eventually going to be married, but there's no reason to rush into anything. We're still young."

"Tch!" Juanita sucked her teeth loudly. "Now, you boys weren't raised to be shackin' up like you don't have good sense."

"We're not shacking up, Aunt Juanita," Luke said, rolling his eyes. "We're just taking our time."

"Don't take too much time…" the older woman advised.

Her husband interrupted. "Woman, don't start. These kids know exactly what they're doing. They'll tie the knot when they're good and ready."

"Good and ready," Luke echoed, shaking his head in agreement.

Juanita rolled her eyes skyward.

Marah laughed. "Juanita's ready to have another wedding!" she exclaimed.

"So, Matthew!" Vanessa interjected as she licked her fingers clean. "How are you and the judge doing?"

Matthew choked on the swallow of coffee he had just put

in his mouth. He coughed to clear his throat before responding. "Excuse me?"

"You and Judge Broomes. How are you two doing?" Vanessa asked, eyeing him curiously. "Are there any wedding bells on the horizon?"

All the women turned to stare at Matthew, each leaning forward in anticipation.

Matthew chuckled softly, his head waving from side to side.

"We're due for another wedding," Marah said coyly, winking an eye at John.

Her husband winked back, a wide grin filling his face.

Matthew's cell phone ringing on his hip interrupted the moment. "Saved by the bell!" he said, rising from his seat. "Excuse me. I need to take this," he said, a smile spreading across his face.

Vanessa laughed. "Tell the judge we said hello!" she said as he made a quick exit out of the room. The rest of the family laughed with her.

Edward shook his head from side to side. "I swear, you all are like a pack of vultures!"

With breakfast completed, Matthew made his way down to the corral as the stable hands were moving his favorite horse from the barn to the work track.

Papa Chico, the elderly Mexican man who'd been with the Briscoe family since forever, tossed his hand up in greeting. "*Buenos días,* Señor Mateo."

"Good morning. How's Champ doing this morning?" Matthew asked as he stroked the horse's muzzle, the massive animal nudging him for attention.

The ranch hand nodded. "He's doing well. Ready to be exercised. Do you want to ride him this morning, señor?"

Matthew shook his head. "Not this morning, sir. Do your thing."

The older man nodded. Grabbing the horse's reins, Papa Chico guided the animal down to the track. Moving down to the fenced field behind them, Matthew leaned against the wooden gate and watched as they prepped Champ to run.

The horse was impressive, heavy on muscle with long legs. Papa Chico started the horse at a slow trot around the track once and then a second time. He picked up the pace with the third lap, the horse moving smoothly through the first furlong. By the time he hit the sixth furlong pole, the mammoth animal was moving as though he was in full control. As Champ rounded the backstretch, his long legs were reaching out for the ground so swiftly that it appeared as though he were just a dark streak blowing in the breeze.

Matthew nodded, satisfaction painting his expression. His investment in the horse was about more than business. His affection for the animal had taken a strong hold on his spirit, and it moved him to see Champ doing so well.

Following the horse and rider back into the barn, Matthew helped unbridle and unsaddle the animal. "He's running really well," he said.

Papa Chico nodded his agreement. "This one's a serious runner, señor. He loves the track. Have you decided if you want to race him or not?"

Matthew nodded. "I have. I agree with you that he's definitely derby material. So, let's schedule him for a few prep races and see how he does."

Papa Chico grinned broadly, excitement gleaming from his dark eyes. *"Si, señor!"*

"And we need to start interviewing jockeys. Whoever is going to ride him needs to come on board early. When you're ready to set up interviews, just call my office and have my secretary clear my schedule."

Nodding, the older man couldn't hide his pleasure. He'd been waiting for this day since the first time he was able to run the horse. Matthew sneaked a hand into his pocket and pulled out a cube of sugar. Sensing he was going to receive a treat, Champ whinnied, his head brushing against Matthew's shoulder. When he'd taken the sugary snack from the palm of his owner's hand, he nuzzled Matthew one more time.

John stepped into the barn as Matthew stood watching the horse being led away. He gestured for his brother's attention. "Hey, do you have a minute?"

Matthew nodded. "For you, big brother, I have two. What's up?"

"Is your passport current?"

"You need to ask?"

John smiled. "I need you to fly to Paris tomorrow. Pierre Demy had a mild heart attack yesterday and is in the hospital. He was smack-dab in the middle of negotiating our import deal with the French Trade Commission. I need you to pick up where he left off."

Matthew nodded, expressing his concern for the senior solicitor in the Stallion Enterprises European offices. "Pierre's doing all right, I hope?"

"He's doing very well. His wife said they anticipate a full recovery, but he needs to take it easy for a few weeks."

Matthew shifted into business mode. "No problem. Pierre has kept me briefed, and I've already reviewed all the contracts. We shouldn't run into any glitches."

"Unless you forget your French and call someone's mother a babbling baboon."

The two brothers laughed heartily.

"My French won't be the problem. *J'ai reçu des A dans toutes mes classes de français, au cas où vous avez oublié.*"

John's laugh echoed across the fields. "No, I didn't forget that you passed your French courses with all As. I remember clearly that you passed French, Spanish and German at the top of your class."

"And please, don't forget I also speak fluent Japanese and

Arabic. So you don't need to be worried about my French. I got it like that," Matthew said, high-fiving his brother.

John grinned. "Show-off!" he muttered, his head waving from side to side.

Matthew laughed with him as they headed back in the direction of the family home. As they approached the back of the house, he paused, coming to a halt.

"What's wrong?" John asked.

"I was just thinking that I should have everything wrapped up by day two. I might take the rest of the week for a little rest and relaxation. Paris is beautiful this time of year."

"Sounds like a plan to me. Paris is even more beautiful with the right woman," John said, his eyebrows raised suggestively.

Matthew cut an eye in his brother's direction, a wide smile blossoming across his dark face. "I was actually thinking the same thing."

"Do you think Katrina will be able to go? I'm assuming, of course, that it's Katrina you want to take with you."

Matthew grinned broadly. "No one else! I know she has a light court calendar this week. Making arrangements for her son might be the only issue."

"That's not a problem," John said. "Collin can stay here at the ranch with us. Marah and I will keep our eye on him. It'll give us some practice."

Matthew raised an eyebrow. "Something you want to tell, big brother?"

John laughed. "Practice for all the babysitting we'll be doing once Mitch and Vanessa have their babies. Nothing more, thank you!"

Matthew grinned. "Well, then, I guess all that's left is convincing my girl to go away with me."

"And knowing your persuasive skills, I don't anticipate you having any problems at all."

Matthew shrugged. "I don't know, John. Katrina's not like any other woman I have ever dated. She's…" Matthew paused.

John stood staring at him, waiting for him to finish his statement. When his brother said nothing, dropping into deep thought, he nodded his head knowingly. "It looks like you might have met a woman who truly challenges you," he said, breaking the silence.

Blowing a gust of warm air past his full lips, Matthew sighed. "Just between me and you," he said, looking over his shoulder to ensure that no one was eavesdropping on their conversation, "the way I'm feeling about Katrina, if all goes well, the girls might get that wedding sooner than they think. And I've never imagined myself thinking about doing something like that."

John grinned, tapping his brother on the back. "I'm happy for you, Matthew. If Katrina brings you half the happiness that Marah has brought me, then you are a very lucky man."

Matthew nodded. "She does and then some. Looks like you're going to have to pay Vanessa another twenty dollars," he said nonchalantly.

John laughed. "Not me. I knew better than to take a fool's bet like that one!"

Chapter 14

Standing at the foot of the bed, staring into an empty suitcase, Katrina looked completely lost. The task of packing for a few days of vacation shouldn't be so daunting, but suddenly she found herself overwhelmed.

Inside her walk-in closet her friend Lacey was chattering nonstop, the woman's enthusiasm bursting at the seams. Lacey poked her head out the door to see if Katrina was still listening to her.

"Did you hear me? This will be the perfect opportunity for you to dust off them cobwebs! It'll be like losing your virginity all over again."

Katrina blushed profusely. "You have completely lost your mind. I don't even know if I should go."

"What do you mean?" Lacey asked as she moved back into the room, a mountain of garments tossed over her arm. "You better go."

"Collin's having issues. He doesn't want to stay at the ranch, plus I have work that needs to be—"

"And there's a full moon on Wednesday and the sky might fall," Lacey said sarcastically. "Damn, Katrina, you can come up with a million and one excuses why you shouldn't go spend a week away with the man of your dreams or you can come up with one absolutely brilliant excuse why you should. I say go with the one, finish packing and head for the airport before he leaves without you. You know you need to shake some of that dust out that chimney of yours!" she added with her eyebrows raised suggestively.

Katrina laughed. "I swear, Lacey, you are such a fool sometimes!"

Lacey laughed with her. "No, I'm honest. You know you want to go. Paris. On a private jet! It's an opportunity that might not come along again anytime soon, so you need to go for it. Collin will get over his issues. He's a teenager. They're never happy about anything."

Lacey shifted gears, holding up a pair of white cotton panties. "Now, do you have anything that the man will want to take off of you slowly and not run from when he sees them? 'Cause these aren't going to work."

Shaking her head from side to side, Katrina sauntered over to her dresser and pulled open the top drawer. Two oversize Victoria's Secret bags lay inside, the familiar pink wrapping moving Lacey to grin broadly.

"Ohhh, what do we have here? You've been keeping secrets. Let me see what you've got there!" she exclaimed excitedly, pulling the bags from Katrina's hand.

Katrina grinned. "Don't hurt yourself, Lacey," she said as her friend held up one item of lingerie after another.

"It's not me I'm worried about," Lacey retorted and laughed. "Looks like you plan to put a hurtin' on your man!" She held up a little black and lace number that would clearly accentuate Katrina's curves and leave little to the imagination.

Katrina snatched the garment out of her best friend's hands.

"I've got this covered, Lacey. I just need some help putting together a few outfits that don't look like I'm going to work, please."

Lacey nodded. "Did you call the stylist I told you about?"

Katrina nodded. "She and I are getting together when I get back. I will get me a whole new wardrobe then."

"Well, it's about time. I've been telling you since forever that you need to improve your style."

"Thank you, Lacey."

Lacey rolled her eyes, dropping down onto the side of the bed as Katrina tossed her lingerie into the suitcase. "No thanks necessary. Just remember to take notes. Paris is seriously for the grown and sexy. If I can't be there myself, I can at least live vicariously through you."

When Katrina arrived at the ranch with Collin in tow, the boy had just about worked her very last nerve. He'd been argumentative and testy since his mother had told him she was going away. He had lost every ounce of his common sense when Katrina made him toss jeans and T-shirts into a duffel bag to get him through the week. As they made their way up the wide steps to the home's large front porch, he was still pouting profusely.

"You need to fix that attitude of yours," Katrina admonished. "I don't know why you have that chip on your shoulder, but I am past ready to knock it right off."

"I don't see why I have to stay here. I'm old enough to stay home by myself. Aunt Lacey could have checked in on me."

"Aunt Lacey is trying a very important case this week. She does not have time to worry about you. Besides, someone is going to have to get you back and forth to school and here to the ranch so that you can stay on your probation schedule. Matthew's brother volunteered, and you need to show some appreciation. I am telling you now, Collin. Do not act like you have never had any home training while I'm gone. You will not be happy if I come back and find out that you've embarrassed me!'"

Collin rolled his eyes at his mother, twisting his face into an annoyed scowl. "Whatever."

Katrina clenched her jaw tightly. She was just about to respond when Marah pulled open the front door and greeted them warmly.

"Katrina, hello. Hi, Collin. Come on in," she said, swinging open the screened door and gesturing for them both to come inside. "Collin, we're so excited that you'll be staying with us."

Collin shrugged his shoulders. "Yeah."

"Katrina, Matthew is back in the family room with the rest of the family. Collin, let me take you upstairs and show you where you'll be staying. Then we'll come back down and catch up with your mother."

"Yes, ma'am," he muttered under his breath.

Katrina watched as her son followed reluctantly behind his host. Standing at the bottom of the stairs, staring, she couldn't help but wonder if taking a trip with Matthew was the right thing for her to do. Matthew called out her name, interrupting her thoughts.

As he moved to her side, gliding an arm around her waist and pulling her close to his body, all her doubt disappeared like vapor.

"Hey," she said, pressing her palms to his chest as she reached to kiss his lips. "How are you?"

"I'm doing remarkably well now that you're here."

A wide smile filled her face. "I'm doing really good, too," she said. "I'll be better once Collin stops acting like the world has come to an end."

Matthew chuckled. "He'll be just fine. My brothers have a full schedule planned for him. In fact, he'll be heading to the race track with Mark tonight. Being down in the pits, up close with the bikes, should brighten his mood considerably."

He wrapped his arms around her torso and hugged her tightly. Leaning his face against hers, he pressed his cheek to her cheek. His eyes were closed as his hands skated down the length of his back. She felt good in his arms, and he would have continued to hold on to her if Marah and Collin hadn't come bounding down the steps in their direction. He reluctantly dropped his arms back to his sides as he took a step back.

"So, you two ready to take off?" Marah asked.

Katrina took a deep breath, filling her lungs with air.

Matthew nodded. "We just need to make sure Collin is settled. How are you doing, buddy?" he asked, turning his attention to the teenager, who was glaring in his direction.

The boy shrugged his narrow shoulders. "Okay, I guess."

Matthew nodded. "Glad to hear it."

Collin rolled his eyes, still scowling. He met his mother's stare. "I don't feel well. I think I have a temperature," he said, feigning a weak cough into the crook of his elbow.

Katrina reached to feel his forehead. "You don't feel warm."

"Well, I am. I'm burning up. I think I'm getting sick."

Katrina cut an eye in Matthew's direction. He winked an eye at her.

"That doesn't sound good," Matthew said, reaching to feel the kid's forehead. "Yeah, you definitely feel a little warm to me." He turned to Katrina. "Maybe we should postpone our trip."

"Who's postponing their trip?" Mark asked, making his way into the foyer to see what was going on. He waved a hand at Katrina, then looked up to say hello to Collin. "So, you about ready to ride, kid?" he asked.

"Ride?" Collin looked confused.

"I'm making time, money. If you're coming to the track with me, we need to head on out."

Matthew shook his head. "Sorry, Mark. Collin seems to be

coming down with something. Doesn't look like he's going to be able to go anywhere tonight."

Mark nodded. "That's a shame, kid. I hear you're a wiz when it comes to an engine."

"Well, it's not that bad," Collin said, a distinct change in his tone. "I just…"

Matthew gestured with his head. "No, we wouldn't want anything to happen to you. Your mom and I would be devastated. We'll just cancel our plans and stay here and look out for you. That's the right thing to do. Don't you think so, Katrina?"

Katrina smiled faintly, her head waving up and down. "Definitely. In fact—" she lifted herself up to the step Collin was standing on "—I think we need to get you to bed right away." She brushed her palm across his forehead.

"Too bad," Mark said, moving in the direction of the front door. "You would have had the best seats in the stadium."

"No!" Collin exclaimed, excited, his voice rising substantially. "Really, I'm feeling better. I can go! Please!"

Katrina shook her head. "Are you sure, son? I wouldn't want to leave and have you go off to the races and then get sick. I'd feel horrible!"

"It's not a problem," Collin said, reaching to kiss her cheek. "Have a good trip," he said as he moved in Mark's direction, heading for the safety helmet the man was extending in his direction.

Before Katrina could respond, her son was out the door and headed down the front steps. As Mark rolled out behind him, he laughed heartily. Looking back over his shoulder, he shook his head at his family and waved goodbye.

Matthew laughed. "Luke pulled the same stunt when he was that age. In fact, he went so far as to use a lighter to heat up the thermometer to make it look like he had a fever."

Marah giggled. "What happened?"

"It took him weeks to figure out why John didn't fall for him having a one-hundred-fifty-three-degree temperature."

They all laughed heartily.

Matthew reached for Katrina's hand. "We need to go, sweetheart. We've got a fourteen-hour flight ahead of us."

Katrina nodded, the warmth from his fingers caressing her flesh. She met Marah's gaze, the other woman eyeing her intently. "Thank you, Marah. I really appreciate your family keeping an eye on Collin for me."

Marah smiled reassuringly. "Don't you worry. Collin is going to be just fine. You just go have a great time," she said. She gave Katrina a sly wink. "A really, really great time!"

Chapter 15

They'd been in the air for hours, talking about everything and about nothing as they passed the time. Katrina lay cradled in Matthew's arms, her legs extended across the airplane's leather upholstery as she stared out the window at the cloud-filled sky.

The Stallion jet had been waiting on the tarmac for them, the flight attendant and pilot ready to meet every one of their needs. Katrina had been slightly taken aback by the attention, but Matthew's nonchalant attitude about flying in a private plane without the hassle of long lines, the baggage check-in and the security checks of commercial flights quickly put her at ease.

From the moment they'd stepped aboard, the two had been completely relaxed, basking easily in the comfort they felt with each other. Matthew drew his fingers down the length of her arm as he nuzzled a kiss against her neck.

"You're a distraction, Judge Broomes," he said softly as he relished the warmth of her skin against his lips.

Katrina giggled ever so softly. "And what, pray tell, makes you say that?" she asked.

"Because I should be brushing up on the details of my contract negotiations, and instead…" He paused, his voice dropping an octave. "Instead, I'm trying to brush up on you."

Katrina couldn't contain the wealth of emotion that bubbled through her spirit. She cuddled closer against Matthew's broad chest as he tightened his arms around her torso. Joy painted her expression, the sheer energy of it gleaming deep in her eyes.

"I have no doubts, Counselor, that you are well versed in all the details of your negotiations, which is why you can afford to be distracted by other things."

He chuckled heartily. "Baby, other *things* is not what I'm distracted by. The sexiest, most beautiful woman in the world has my full and undivided attention."

"Is that so?"

"Yes, ma'am. She's got me so wound up that I don't know if I'm coming or going most of the time."

"That sounds very personal."

Matthew nodded, planting a damp kiss on her cheek. "It's become very serious."

"Hmmm," Katrina purred softly. She cut an eye up at him, smiling sweetly. "Thank you for inviting me. I was reluctant to come at first, but I'm looking forward to our having a great time."

"My lady, I can guarantee you will have the most memorable week of your life."

Nodding her head against his chest, she didn't have anything else to say. All she wanted was to stop time and enjoy the moment.

Katrina lounged in a tub of warm water. For the first time in two days she felt normal again, her body having adjusted to the difference in time and the serious jet lag having finally subsided. Matthew had called and asked her to be ready for a late dinner, his business dealings successfully concluded. He wanted to celebrate the major coup for the Stallion family business, and he wanted to celebrate with her.

After an absolutely delightful day Katrina decided she loved Paris best in the early mornings, before the city had fully woken up. The Pont Neuf, the oldest bridge in Paris, had become one of her favorite places, the views absolutely magnificent. Watching the sun rise over the horizon that morning had been positively enchanting. She had visited the typical tourist haunts and then had stepped away from those areas and had discovered quaint residential streets, quiet wood-paneled cafés, old bookshops and marvelous art galleries. Not having Matthew with her had been the day's only imperfection. When they had last spoken, he had promised to make that up to her. Katrina had plans for him, as well, logistics of such having taken some maneuvering.

Easing her way out of the Jacuzzi tub, Katrina wrapped an oversize plush white towel around her naked form. Taking a quick glance at the timepiece that rested on the bathroom counter, she mused that she had at least an hour before Matthew would be returning to the hotel. Always the consummate gentleman, he had booked separate accommodations at the luxury hotel. The suite he'd situated her in was a three-bedroom extravaganza that put her own home to shame. Matthew had taken up residence in the adjoining suite, a single door standing between them.

The first night they'd both passed out from exhaustion, Katrina in her suite and Matthew in his. He was gone when she awoke the next morning, business superseding everything else. Katrina had slept most of the day away. When Matthew had returned, he'd been in full lawyer mode, focused solely on business and what he needed to do to accomplish what he'd come all the way across the Atlantic to accomplish. Knowing the importance of that, Katrina had taken a step back, moving herself well out of his way so as not to interfere.

When it was time to settle down for the night, Matthew fell asleep on the living-room sofa in her suite, legal documents scattered around him. Katrina had watched him as he slept, his head tossed back, his mouth open ever so slightly. He snored. Softly. The sound of it was almost calming as he sucked in air and blew it out in a deep, low whistle. When she could no longer keep her own eyes open, Katrina had curled up on the opposite end of the sofa, wrapping a cashmere blanket around both of them. When she awoke, he was gone and a single red rose rested on the sofa cushion beside her. And now, finished with his business, he had promised her his full and undivided attention for the rest of the week. Deep in thought, Katrina had promised him something, as well. Matthew just didn't know it yet.

Back in one of the suite's luxurious bedrooms Katrina slipped into a pair of black lace panties and a matching bra. Sliding black nylons up the length of her legs, she stepped into a pair of black, four-inch stilettos. Standing in front of the full-length mirror, she took in her reflection, pleased with what she saw. Diligent exercise had her body firm and toned. Her skin was soft and supple, and she routinely slathered on a thick layer of moisturizer to keep it that way. Debating whether to wear her hair up or down, Katrina opted for down, allowing the lush blue-black strands to curl ever so slightly against her shoulders. A shimmer of blush across her cheeks, dark liner beneath her eyes and a hint of gloss on her lips were her only makeup. By the time Matthew knocked on the door for her, she had zipped up her sleek black lace dress and was feeling quite pleased with herself.

Matthew's full grin was approving when she pulled open the door to allow him inside. With his arms crossed over his chest, he leaned against the door frame. His gaze skated from the top of her head down to the leather shoes that adorned her feet and back again.

"Hey, honey, I'm home!" he chimed easily. A soft chuckle eased past her lips. Matthew leaned to kiss her cheek, allowing his lips to linger against her skin as he inhaled the delicate scent of her perfume. He wrapped his arms around her torso and hugged her tightly. "You look stunning," he said, nodding his head.

Katrina smiled back. "Thank you!"

"Ready to go have some fun?" Matthew asked as he clasped her hand beneath his.

She nodded, her exuberant expression answering for her.

Matthew gestured toward the door. "Your chariot awaits, my lady."

The whole of Paris was enchanting and romantic. A car and driver were waiting outside the hotel for them, ready to whisk them off to wherever Matthew directed. And first he commanded that they be taken to Le Pré Catelan, Paris's most prestigious restaurant. The elegant eatery was nestled in a tranquil, luxuriant area deep in the heart of the Bois de Boulogne, only a few minutes from the Champs-Elysées.

Katrina had grown used to everyone knowing and fawning over Matthew Stallion. The restaurant's staff greeted him as if he dined there every day of the week, attentive to his every need, even before he asked. Matthew ordered their meals, lavishing her with the most incredible French cuisine and wines selected by one of the most respected sommeliers in the city. Matthew had greeted the man warmly, and the two were pleased to be reacquainted with one another.

"Olivier Poussier is an old friend," he said, extolling the wine steward's many virtues. "Olivier's creative expertise is renowned."

"Do you come here often?" Katrina asked.

He nodded. "I've been known to fly in for dinner when the moment moves me."

"You just fly to Paris for dinner?"

"And dessert," Matthew said, his voice dropping seductively.

The deep tone sent a shiver up Katrina's spine, moving her to press her knees together tightly to stall the heat that had erupted at the cusp between her thighs.

After the meal, Matthew held her hand, leading her out of the restaurant and back to the waiting car.

"There's a wonderful little club not too far from here. The jazz is soft and the wine is exceptional. We can dance cheek to cheek until the sun comes up. You game?"

Katrina met his deep gaze. A smile pulled at the corners of her mouth. "Why don't we save that for tomorrow? I actually thought we'd do something different tonight."

Matthew lifted his brows, curiosity washing over his expression. "And what might that be, beautiful lady?"

Katrina's smile was intriguing. "We need to go back to the hotel first. I forgot something," she said, pausing ever so slightly. "Then I'll tell you."

Matthew nodded, sensing that she wasn't going to give him any more information as she slid into the vehicle. He followed, close on her heels, instructing the driver to return them to their home away from home.

As the chauffeur pulled in front of the hotel's entrance, Katrina pressed her palm to his knee and squeezed it gently. "Wait here," she said softly. "I won't be long."

"I can walk up with you," Matthew said, moving to exit the car with her.

Katrina pressed her palm to his chest and gently pushed him back against his seat. She winked an eye. "Not necessary," she said. "It will only take a quick minute. I'll call if I need your help."

"Hurry back," Matthew said, reaching to give her a quick kiss. "I miss you already."

Inside the hotel's lobby, the concierge waved in her direction. "Mademoiselle Broomes, everything is as you requested. Is there anything else that I can assist you with tonight?"

Waving her head from side to side, Katrina took a deep inhale of air. "Thank you, but I can't think of anything else."

The man nodded as Katrina smiled her appreciation. She headed for the elevators and went up to the penthouse suite. Opening the door, she stepped inside and took in the view. It couldn't be more perfect. Dialing the room's telephone, she asked the operator to connect her to Matthew Stallion. As his cell phone rang on the other end, she suddenly found herself nervous, second-guessing what she had planned as anxiety rustled deep in her midsection.

"Hello?"

"Hey," Katrina said softly.

"Is everything okay?" Matthew asked, concern rising in his voice.

Katrina smiled into the receiver. "Everything is perfect, but I could use some assistance, after all."

"No problem," Matthew intoned. "I'll be right up."

"Oh, and one more thing," Katrina added. "Tell the driver we won't need him anymore tonight."

Matthew paused, his curiosity seriously piqued. "Are you sure?"

Katrina giggled softly. "Absolutely positive."

Dismissing the driver, Matthew exited the parked vehicle and rushed through the hotel lobby. The concierge greeted him cheerfully, gesturing for his attention.

"Monsieur Stallion, a moment please, sir."

Not wanting to be detained, Matthew barely hesitated.

"Please, sir. It's very important," the concierge persisted.

"Yes?"

The concierge extended his hand and gave Matthew a passkey to an unfamiliar room. "Sir, mademoiselle has asked that you please join her in the penthouse gardens." The man smiled politely, his expression revealing nothing more than what his duties required.

A look of confusion washed over Matthew's face. Nodding his gratitude, he turned abruptly and rushed toward the elevators, his focus on nothing else but reaching Katrina to see what was going on. He didn't have a clue what she could possibly be up to, but he was seriously intrigued.

He hated that she'd had to spend her first days in Paris alone. He was intent on making up for every minute. He was anxious to show her everything he loved about the city and even more intent on the two of them discovering their own favorite places and things together.

As the elevator reached the rooftop floor, he moved quickly to the door of the suite. Using the passkey, he let himself inside. His excitement was almost consuming.

The interior was dimly lit, and it seemed as if no one was there. Matthew called out Katrina's name, moving forward into the large suite, eagerly searching for her. Katrina's faint voice called out to him, moving him to follow the sound. As he came to the glass doors that led out to the rooftop gardens, Matthew's eyes widened in surprise. He came to a quick halt, and then a wide grin spread like wildfire across his face.

Chapter 16

The lush landscape of the rooftop gardens featured white and lavender spray roses, full-size gerbera daisies, trailing lantana, verdant hydrangea, dense evergreens, wisteria, which covered arched trellises, and twinkling white lights, which cast a romantic glow against the dark sky. A king-size bed adorned in luxurious white bedding sat in the center of the space. And smack-dab in the center of the bed, Katrina reclined in nothing but black lace. The view was magnificent.

Suddenly unnerved, Matthew tossed a quick glance over his left shoulder before stepping through the glass doors. He felt as if he'd fallen into the rabbit hole, completely lost in the looking glass of his very own private Garden of Eden. The moment was almost surreal, and Matthew suddenly prayed that if it all were a dream, he do nothing that would render him awake anytime soon.

Katrina's coquettish expression was teasing. She smiled seductively, biting down against her bottom lip. Her eyes narrowed ever so slightly as she crooked her index finger and gestured for him to come to her. Time seemed to stand still as Matthew slowly closed the short expanse of space between them. He came to a halt at the foot of the bed, his gaze locked with hers. Never before had he seen anything more beautiful.

Katrina was the epitome of elegance and grace. She was also quite the temptress as she pursed her lips in a seductive pout, her tongue peeking ever so slightly past her lips. Her haunting eyes were luring him into a deep spell, and Matthew could feel himself losing full and total control to her. The intensity of the moment was almost unbearable. It felt as if a torch had ignited beneath his feet, the wealth of heat causing him to break out in a cold sweat. An erection lengthened like a steel rod between his legs, the weight of it pressing tight against his inner pant leg.

Moving up on her knees, Katrina crawled toward him. She extended her hand out to touch his upper thigh. Her fingers slid slowly up to his waist and the black leather belt that held up his slacks. She continued her climb until she could wrap her arms around his neck, her torso pressing tight to his. He could feel the protrusion of her nipples pressing against his chest, the rock-hard candies teasing him even more.

Katrina pressed her mouth to his, kissing him hungrily. The urgency of it took his breath away. The connection felt like forever, neither one of them wanting to let go. When she finally drew back, he met her gaze, every ounce of his emotion still swimming in her dark eyes.

"Very nice," Matthew muttered against her lips, his warm breath blowing against her skin. "Very, very, very nice."

Katrina purred softly, the low hum like a mating call commanding his full and undivided attention. Matthew pulled at the knot that held his necktie in place, loosening it and the top buttons of his dress shirt. Katrina smiled seductively, her hands moving his out of the way as she finished unbuttoning the rest of the pearl-toned buttons to expose his broad chest. A light tuft of black hair peppered the expanse of dark chocolate skin. Katrina drew her fingers over the strands, her manicured nails caressing him gingerly. Her lips followed, trailing damp kisses across his flesh. Matthew shivered, a rush of cold shimmying up his spine.

He dipped his head down and, before she could protest, kissed her. It was gentle at first, flesh lightly caressing flesh, and then Katrina opened her mouth to him, searching out his tongue with her own. Matthew felt as if a volcano had erupted, waves of heat washing down over the two of them.

He clasped her face between the palms of his hands, his thumbs caressing each of her cheeks. Katrina reached a palm around the back of his neck, her fingers stroking the nape of his neck, deepening the kiss.

Before he realized it, Matthew had lost his clothes, his shirt and necktie discarded on the floor. Moments later the barrier that was their clothing proved too much for them both, and they gave in to the urgent need to feel skin against skin fueled by ravenous desire. Katrina had pulled at the zipper of his slacks and had loosened his belt to free him. Belt and pants were tangled around his feet. His erection tented the front of his silk boxers. There was no denying the obvious yearning that had surged with a vengeance between them.

"You know you're torturing me, don't you?" Matthew said, wrapping his arms tightly around her torso.

Katrina hugged him close, enjoying the sensation of his broad chest pressing tight to her breasts, her nipples kissing him through the sheer lace bra she wore. She laughed softly. The lilt of it was intoxicating, and he felt as if he would come out of his skin if he couldn't have her.

She pressed her hands to his shoulders, silently urging him to sit down on the edge of the bed. The excitement was almost too much for Matthew to bear, and he felt his manhood twitch in anticipation, his heartbeat throbbing in the length of flesh.

As she pulled him back against the mattress top, all he could think of was how much he wanted her. He slid his arms around her thin waist, his hands cupping the cheeks of her ass as his mouth laid claim to hers. The feel of Katrina reclined against him was intense, and she moaned her own pleasure against his full lips. He slid his hands up the length of her back, kneading and caressing her warm flesh. He tugged at the clasp to her bra, the hooks tearing from the fabric. One hand snaked into the length of her hair, tangling with the strands as he continued the ardent kiss. Their tongues were tangled, as well, and both of them felt as if they had stopped breathing.

Katrina drew back to take a deep breath, and as Matthew blew a gust of air out of his own lungs, she locked her gaze with his. Both were panting heavily as she kissed a path along his jawline, over the curve of his dimpled cheeks, up to his forehead and down to the tip of his nose. She nipped lightly at his ear, flicking her tongue along the curve of his earlobe before plunging it deep into his ear canal.

Matthew moaned loudly, the sound vibrating through the late-night air. His body quivered with pure, unadulterated lust. He shifted beneath her until Katrina was straddling him, her legs wrapped around his thighs, the cushion of her mons tight against his throbbing organ.

Snatching what was left of her brassiere from around her, Matthew cupped both of her breasts, running his thumbs across her nipples. Katrina reciprocated with a slow grind of her pelvis against his protruding member. Lifting himself up, Matthew sucked one rock-candy nipple into his mouth as his fingers teased the other. Katrina clutched at him, throwing her head back as her nails dug into his flesh. As he suckled one breast and then the other, a wave of electric spasms pulsated through her body.

Katrina suddenly wanted him more than she had ever wanted any man. The wanting actually hurt, the ache of it the sweetest sensation she'd ever known. She imagined that if Matthew didn't touch her any more that night, she would combust, the heat swelling within her so intense that it literally took her breath away. She was panting heavily, and Matthew seemed to sense her desperation.

He hugged her tightly, pressing his face into her neck as he muttered her name against her skin. With a quick spin, Katrina found herself on her back, Matthew hovering above her, his weight resting on his forearms. He leaned in to give her a quick kiss before pulling his body upward and away. A wave of cool air wafted between them, and Katrina didn't like anything about the sensation. She wanted his heat, Stallion heat, and she wanted it right then.

"Where are you going?" she asked as she reached a hand out to draw him back to her.

Matthew smiled, a broad grin filling his face. "Baby, I'm not going anywhere," he said with a soft chuckle as he reached for his suit jacket and the leather billfold concealed in the inner pocket. When he drew his hand back, a gold-foiled condom rested in his palm.

Dipping his hands into the waistband of his boxers, Matthew slid them over his hips, dropped them to his feet and kicked them out of his way. Katrina's mouth dropped open, her eyes widening in sheer awe. She lifted her eyes to his. His expression teasing, he shifted his gaze downward and she followed it, noticing the significant length of manhood between his legs twitching for attention.

As he dropped back down on the bed, tearing at the wrapper to expose the prophylactic inside, Katrina couldn't resist taking him into the palm of her hand. The elongated organ was a thing of sheer beauty, a luscious dark chocolate lollipop, pure, delectable candy. She shifted her gaze to his face and saw that Matthew sat with his eyes closed tight, pleasure washing over his expression as she stroked him. She pushed and pulled at him, enjoying the feel of him in her hand. He was rock hard, of substantial size, and seemed to grow even larger under her ministrations.

Pressing a palm into the center of his chest, Katrina pushed Matthew down on the bed, pulling the condom from his fingers. As he watched, amusement dancing in his eyes, she sheathed him slowly.

Reaching for his hand, Katrina braced herself as she lifted her body above his. As he stared up at her, his lustful expression danced with hers. Her breasts swayed for attention just out of his reach, and when he lifted his torso to grasp them, Katrina lifted her foot and pushed him back down against the mattress. Her manicured toes tapped lightly against his chest as she allowed her foot to rest there. Matthew grinned broadly.

Katrina refused to wait one more minute. She'd waited too many years for an opportunity to be with a man who had her heart and soul. She wanted Matthew to know her like no other man since her late husband had known her.

Easing her lace panties down, she stepped out of them, balancing herself cautiously on one foot, and then the other, as Matthew's extended arms kept her from falling. Sliding down, Katrina straddled his body, and when her pelvis was just millimeters from meeting his, Matthew slipped one hand between her legs, the other clasping her buttocks. Her breath caught deep in her throat as he teased her femininity, his fingers dancing a waltz against her most private place. His touch was heated, the lingering strokes making her moist.

Her breathing erratic, she dropped her torso on his. She could feel herself about to explode, the sensation so intense that Katrina wanted to scream out loud. With no other thought, she lifted herself slightly above the erection that was dancing at the door to her secret garden, then plunged her body down hard against his, wrapping her flesh tight around his. The moment was sheer magic.

When Matthew felt himself glide deep into Katrina, the satin softness of her body like a vise clamp caressing every inch of him, his mind turned to incoherent mush. His body was awash with flames, nerve endings erupting with each stroke and grind against his pelvis. The sensations were overwhelming, rocketing him skyward. Unable to contain himself, he lifted his hips to meet her thrusts as she rode his manhood.

Stroke for stroke the couple savored the intense sensations. Lifting his torso, Matthew sat upright, wrapping his arms tightly around her. Katrina clutched him tightly as he grabbed her buttocks with one hand, the other hand gliding the length of her back as she rocked against him. Slipping his fingers into her hair, he teased the nape of her neck as he kissed her, his tongue sliding against hers.

Grabbing her knees, Matthew shifted her legs until they were wrapped tightly around his waist. With both of his hands he pushed and pulled at her behind, gliding himself in and out of her body. His expression was one of pure ecstasy.

Air caught deep in Katrina's chest. It felt as if they were climbing a mountain, the apex just an arm's length away. Together she and Matthew raced to the summit, anxious to throw themselves into a free fall, and then everything exploded, both their bodies bursting with sheer joy. As they climaxed together, holding tightly to each other, Katrina screamed his name and Matthew chanted hers over and over again.

The sun had begun a slow ascent into the early morning sky. The temperate morning air hinted at a pleasant day on the horizon, sunshine and warmth on order for the day. Matthew lay sprawled across the mattress, staring up through the lush landscape to the sky above. Beside him, Katrina slept soundly, her naked body curled against his, her head cradled in the crook of his arm. She appeared comfortable and content, the hint of a smile pulling at her lush lips, and the sight of her brought a smile to his own face.

Matthew shifted onto his side. Still in the throes of slumber, Katrina seemed to sense his movement and she shifted with him as he wrapped his body around hers. He looped an arm over her waist and pulled her tightly to him, her buttocks snuggled in the curve of his crotch. Her nakedness pressed against his own sent a shiver of heat through his groin, a morning erection springing to life.

He chuckled softly, amused that there was any life at all left in his body. He and Katrina had made love over and over for hours, exploring every nook and crevice of each other's bodies. After he'd pulled the last condom from his pocket, they had opened a new box Katrina had purchased specifically for the two of them and had proceeded to christen the velvet-upholstered chaise in the other room. Matthew didn't think any corner of the sizable suite had gone unexplored.

With a gentle hand he brushed away the spray of hair that had fallen over her shoulder. Nuzzling his face into her neck, he pressed a damp kiss against the soft flesh, allowing his lips to linger there as he blew warm breath against her skin. Katrina snuggled closer to his touch, grinding her buttocks against his rising member.

Slinking down the length of her body, Matthew pressed kisses across the expanse of her back, the length of her arm, her elbow and the curve above her buttocks. Katrina opened her eyes slowly, relishing the warmth of his touch, which was pulling her from her sleep. Memories of her night with Matthew flashed through her mind like snapshots taken with a digital camera. They were vivid and exciting, and as Matthew kissed and then nipped at one butt cheek and then the other, she felt a familiar tingling starting to dance in her feminine quadrant.

"Good morning," she said softly, a low moan easing past her lips.

Matthew nipped her other cheek, then slowly licked the spot where he had bitten. "Yes, it is," he said, his voice a loud whisper.

Matthew nudged her, moving her to roll over onto her back

as he lifted her leg up and over his head. He kissed and nib-
bled at the soft tissue of her inner thighs. Katrina was fully
awake now, naked and wanting, as she lay spread before him.
Anticipation blanketed her body, heat rushing through each
one of her nerve endings. She wanted him to taste her, and
she said so, imploring him to touch her before she exploded.

Matthew teased her instead, still slowly brushing his lips
over her skin, his tongue drawing little circles on her inner
thighs. She opened herself wider, bending her knees ever so
slightly as she spread her legs open even more.

Matthew shifted his body up, sliding right between her
thighs. Katrina had risen up on her elbows, eyeing him anxiously, and he met her gaze, his stare teasing. Leaning forward, he flicked the tip of his tongue across the swollen nub,
causing Katrina to cry out from the touch. Matthew grinned
widely as he looked up to see her toss her head back. He
moved his attention back to her skin, biting gently against the
hollow of her pelvis. Katrina slid her hands along the sides of
his head and arched into him, silently begging him to return
to the wetness between her thighs.

Resisting the temptation, Matthew pulled back, lifting
one leg to kiss the back of her knee and then the other. He
dropped her legs over his shoulders as he crawled back up her
body. When his broad chest pressed against her throbbing love
button, Katrina's breath caught deep in her chest. His hands
pushed against her inner thighs, spreading her open even farther, and then he pushed his tongue into her belly button and
gave it a slight swirl. Katrina wiggled anxiously beneath him,
and he smiled, his mouth still pressed against her skin.

Katrina murmured his name, calling him as if in prayer.
The tension in her body was winding tighter and tighter as
his lips moved up her torso until he reached her breasts. His
tongue lapped at both her nipples, sending a wave of pleasure straight through her. He tightened his lips around her
nipple and suckled eagerly. It was almost too much as she felt

her whole body give way, her hands clutching the sheet beneath them. His tongue was hot, the nipple caught between his teeth, and she moaned loudly, her hips thrusting up hard against him. As she did, Matthew slid a hand between their two bodies, his fingers slipping past the petals of her secret garden to burrow deep inside her. He stroked her inner walls, and Katrina could feel herself contracting like a vise around his fingers as she ground her pelvis against his palm.

Matthew began a slow retreat down her body, planting a trail of delicate kisses against her skin. Katrina's movements became more erratic with each pass of his tongue, her body quivering with excitement.

As he settled back between her legs, guiding her thighs back over his shoulders, Katrina felt as if she were about to implode, the sweltering heat simmering inside her about to combust. It was almost too much to handle. "Oh, Matthew," she gasped through clenched teeth.

Katrina glistened in the early morning light, beads of wetness moistening her feminine petals. Taking in the sight of her, Matthew felt his erection stiffen more, and suddenly he wanted to taste her. Leaning in, he caught the essence of her nectar on his tongue. Katrina cried out as he pushed forward, thrusting his tongue deep inside of her. She lifted her legs even higher, her hips automatically tilting up to give him better access. Her hands pressed against the mattress top as she pushed herself even farther into his mouth. She planted her feet against the top of his shoulders as he serviced her with his tongue, the wave of sensations overwhelming.

Lifting herself back up on her elbows, she eyed him with a narrowed gaze. She wanted to say something, but her words were lost. Katrina couldn't focus on anything but the tremors of sheer passion sweeping through her.

Matthew buried his face between her thighs, his tongue thrusting into her as deeply as he could manage. Katrina was moaning in sync with his tongue, her words incoherent to him. Matthew could sense that she was ready to fall off that edge and so he pulled back. Katrina's juices painted his face, moisture beading on the new facial hair that had sprouted above his lip and beneath his chin.

Katrina lifted her hips in frustration, her body pleading for release. A smug smile filled Matthew's face as he dropped his mouth back down on her, his tongue dancing against her core.

He sucked at her, hard, encircling her waist with his arm to hold her in place as she tried to pull back from the intense sensations he was causing. Her moans were louder as she tried desperately to pull away, her body shaking under the onslaught of his tongue. She could feel herself climbing higher, getting closer to that ledge, the motions of his mouth increasing in speed and pressure.

Katrina began to claw at the bedclothes, tangling the sheet between her fingers. She wanted to pull away, to push closer, anything and everything. And then Matthew pushed his fingers inside of her, tickling that special spot. Her entire body arched up hard against him as the first waves of her orgasm hit, and then she screamed, a low, throaty, husky cry reaching to kiss the rising morning sun.

Chapter 17

Katrina's body was still quivering in Matthew's arms. She was completely spent, barely coherent. She nestled closer to him, wrapping her arms around his waist and locking her hands together behind his back. She'd been drowning in sheer pleasure, and he felt like the lifeline she couldn't live without. She didn't want to ever let him go. Pressing her face into his chest, she kissed him sweetly.

"Did I say good morning?" Matthew muttered as he kissed her forehead.

Katrina laughed. "I think you did. Yes, I do believe you did, Mr. Stallion. You said it quite nicely, as a matter of fact."

Matthew chuckled with her. "I'm glad you approve. I do aim to please, ma'am!"

"You done good, baby. You done real good!"

Matthew gave her a tight squeeze, hugging her warmly. "And now we need to get moving. I've got a full day planned for us."

Katrina's eyes opened widely. "Relaxing right here would be perfectly fine with me."

He smiled, a wide grin filling the expanse of his face. "It will be a day of relaxation, my darling, just not here." He tapped her lightly on her behind. "We need to get a move on it. Look," he said, pointing skyward. "The sun's already up. The day will be gone before we know it."

Brushing her hand across his chest and down the length of his torso, she cupped a palm over his crotch and gave a gentle squeeze. His semierect member twitched beneath her hand. "Wouldn't you rather we just stay and—" she paused, cutting her eye at him "—play?"

Matthew laughed warmly, gripping her wrist to remove her hand. He kissed her cheek. "I promise, baby, we'll have plenty of time to play later."

Katrina pouted, feigning disappointment. She heaved a deep sigh. "I owe you, Mr. Stallion," she said, her eyebrows raised suggestively.

Matthew's grin widened. "Yes, you do and I will collect," he said. He lifted his body from the bed, stretching the length of his limbs upward. "In fact," he said, extending his hand toward her, "since you want to get a late start, why don't we take this conversation to the shower. I could use some help washing my back."

Katrina smiled, her expression coy. "Just your back?"

With raised eyebrows, Matthew gave her a quick wink of his eye as he turned to exit the room. Watching the seductive sway of his broad back and high behind, Katrina felt a newly familiar twinge of heat igniting deep within her. As he tossed her a quick glance over his shoulder, she hopped quickly out of the bed and hurried to catch up to him. She was looking forward to a really good shower.

They took the train from Gare Saint-Lazare to the quaint village of Vernon. Staring out the train's windows, Katrina was awed by the wheat and sunflower fields that rolled past. In Vernon Matthew rented a bicycle built for two for them to ride to Monet's garden in the town of Giverny. The weather was picture-perfect, the moderate temperatures and bright sunshine highlights of the day.

Katrina waved her head from side to side. "Do you know how long it's been since I last rode a bicycle?" she asked as Matthew easily straddled the front, gesturing for her to get on behind him.

"It's like making love, baby," he said. He winked his eye. "Once you get back on, you remember how to ride."

She laughed, not missing the smug expression on his face or the innuendo in his tone. "That's not my problem," she said as a hint of red blossomed across her cheeks.

Matthew nodded his head knowingly. He chuckled softly. "I don't know what I was thinking," he said, reaching for her hand and pulling her to him. He hugged her tightly, planting a damp kiss against her cheek. "Would you prefer we do something else?" he asked.

Katrina shrugged her shoulders. "No, it's not that bad," she said, her cheeks still raging with color.

Their antics had left her a bit tender in her nether regions, the juncture between her thighs having gotten quite a work-out. It had been somewhat of a challenge for her to slip into her denim jeans and walk comfortably after the intense exercise she'd gotten. Even the simple act of walking had proven to be comical, and despite the hilarity of it, Matthew had been exceptionally tender with her. Bike riding, however, had not been on her list of the top ten things to do before she had completely recovered. She hugged him close, her arms wrapped around his neck and back. She laughed gingerly, her head waving from side to side.

Matthew laughed with her. "Are you blushing?"

"Are you teasing me?"

"Of course!"

"Then I must be blushing," she said, mirth bubbling up from her midsection.

Matthew leaned back to give her another quick kiss. "We make beautiful love together, and you hadn't done that in a while, either, but you caught up just like a pro. I'm sure with a little ingenuity we can make this work, too."

He lifted himself off the bike and held up his index finger, gesturing for her to give him a quick minute. Katrina watched as he disappeared inside a cottage drugstore. Minutes later he returned with a small padded whoopee cushion in hand.

Katrina burst out laughing, tears misting her eyes.

"See," Matthew said assuredly, "I am a Boy Scout ready at all times. So, you just let me lead and we won't have any problems. I promise," he said as he tied the cushion securely to the rear seat of the bicycle. He straddled the bike for a second time and gave her a sly wink of his eye.

Taking him at his word, Katrina climbed aboard, holding tight to the handlebars as Matthew pushed them off with his foot and began to pedal.

The ride was sweet as they slowly navigated their way through the streets. Katrina found the experience quite liberating as she pedaled behind Matthew, her minor discomfort practically forgotten. Along the way they stopped at a local food market and picked up a freshly baked baguette, a round of Boursin cheese and a bottle of red wine. Matthew picked the perfect spot along the banks of the Seine River for them to break for lunch. They took a rest on a wooden bench that sat below an old mill, and their time together was idyllic.

In Giverny Katrina felt as if she'd stepped into the canvas of her favorite impressionist painting. With its plethora of colorful flowers, the landscape in Monet's garden was beyond breathtaking. Her favorite spot was the famous Japanese bridge covered with wisteria. Weeping willows and bamboo surrounded the structure, and water lilies bloomed atop the pond below. Katrina knew that bridge would forever remain in her memories, because Matthew had held her hand as they'd strolled across it, stopping dead center to pull her into his arms and kiss her as if he were kissing her for the very first time. It had taken her breath away.

Neither said a word as they rode back on the train. Katrina snuggled down into Matthew's arms and drifted off into a light sleep. He kissed her forehead gently as he scanned the landscape outside the window. The day had been perfect, and he was completely enamored with the woman who slept so soundly in his arms. Closing his eyes, he dropped his head into her hair and dozed lightly with her.

The couple had managed to be in Paris for Museum Night. The all-nighter in the Paris museums happened only once a year. The museums all over the city stayed open all night long for the free event. It was only the second time that Matthew was able to enjoy the experience, and he was thrilled to share it with Katrina.

Behaving as though they were European, the two enjoyed a late-night dinner and then stayed out even later. After another delectable meal, they took a leisurely stroll on Île Saint-Louis, savoring cones filled with chocolate ice cream from Berthillon. Then they went to the Musée Rodin to enjoy the collection of works by the celebrated French sculptor.

"Rodin's works are some of my favorite!" Matthew exclaimed excitedly as they maneuvered their way around Auguste Rodin's *The Kiss,* a marble sculpture of a couple locked in a deep embrace.

"It's masterful," Katrina answered, resisting the temptation to run her hand along the marble pair. "I also like the works done by Camille Claudel. She had quite an eye for the human form, as well. Some of her works are very similar to Rodin's in spirit, but they have an imagination and lyricism of their own."

Matthew nodded. "Claudel was one of Rodin's protégés.

The two apparently had quite a torrid love affair. She was eighteen years old to his forty-three. Sometime after the affair ended, she had a nervous breakdown and was institutionalized. Her family never let her return home."

"That's so sad," Katrina declared, drifting off into thought. "The poor woman had a broken heart, and it was held against her." Her expression was thoughtful with a hint of vulnerability.

"Have you ever had a broken heart, Katrina?" Matthew was moved to ask.

She met Matthew's stare. A slight smile pulled at the edges of her mouth. "In the sixth grade I was head over heels for a boy named Daniel Davis. I made the mistake of telling him how I felt, and I found out he was hard for my best friend, Lorrie. I was crushed.

"But that didn't compare to what it felt like when Collin's father died. The day I received the news that he'd been killed, I was devastated. Then I was angry. I felt like he'd abandoned me. Even though it was totally irrational, I couldn't let it go. It was not a good feeling."

Matthew reached out a hand to touch her cheek, his fingers caressing her face. She dropped her gaze to the floor.

From the Rodin museum they went on to enjoy the scenery at the Palais de la Porte Dorée Tropical Aquarium, with its many tanks of diverse aquatic flora and fauna. The aquatic display was one of the most spectacular that Katrina had ever seen.

At two o'clock in the morning both Katrina and Matthew were still wide-eyed and awake. Holding tight to her hand, Matthew found a secluded little spot in a public garden, and they sat together on one of the garden benches. After their day together he was intent on just holding tight to his woman and whispering sweet nothings in her ear.

Under the moonlit sky, Matthew wrapped his arms around Katrina's torso. She reclined against him as they sat staring at the late-night sky. It had become his most favorite pastime, the two of them relaxing together. With Katrina secure in his arms, Matthew felt as though he'd found his way home, even though he hadn't been lost. All was well in his world, and he couldn't imagine his future without her. He hugged her closer.

"Are you ready to go back to the hotel?" Katrina questioned, breaking the lengthy silence that had fallen over the two of them.

Matthew shook his head. "No, not really. I'm a little hyper. How about yourself?"

She smiled. "I'm wide-awake, as well, and quite comfortable."

Matthew nodded, his mind suddenly racing. "I have an idea," he said as he pulled his cell phone from his pocket and dialed. The French he spoke when the line was answered on the other end was completely lost on Katrina. He spoke French beautifully and it was like the sweetest serenade for her ears, but she didn't have a clue what he was saying to the party on the other end.

Minutes later he had pulled her up by the hand and was leading her to a waiting car that had come directly for them.

"Where are we going?" she asked curiously.

Matthew's coy smile caused a ripple to travel up her spine. "It's a surprise," he said, winking an eye in her direction. "I just happen to have thought of a wonderful place for us to watch the sun rise."

Thirty minutes later Katrina's eyes widened in surprise and confusion. Through the vehicle's dark tinted windows she watched a crew of many as they stood in a vast field and prepped something she couldn't quite identify at first. It was only when they shifted their bodies to the side that she realized it was one of ten hot air balloons being inflated.

An oversize basket was lying on its side, an abundance of colorful nylon spread out over the ground beside it. Two men were holding open the mouth of the balloon as a third blew cold air into it with a fan. As it started to rise, another member of the crew, who, Katrina would later learn, was their pilot, stepped inside the partially inflated balloon, visibly checking the operational lines, the rigging and the pulleys.

Stepping out of the car behind Matthew, Katrina was clearly intrigued. "How cool is this!" she muttered softly under her breath.

Matthew squeezed her hand and winked his eye a second time. Within a span of sixty seconds the balloon was filled to capacity, rising high above the basket that it was attached to. The crew was steadily monitoring its lift, holding it steady downwind to prevent it from toppling over. It was all fascinating to watch, and Katrina's excitement was steadily mounting.

"Have you done this before?" she asked, pressing her palm to Matthew's abdomen.

He nodded. "Many, many years ago. My brother John brought me, Mark and Luke to Paris for Luke's eighteenth birthday. We all went on a ride to celebrate. It was fun!"

"Is it scary? I mean, I'm not a big fan of heights!" She giggled softly.

Matthew laughed with her. "Don't you worry. I'll be right here holding on to you the whole time. I won't let anything happen," he said as he wrapped her in a deep bear hug.

In no time at all, the pilot was gesturing for them to get on board. A wave of anxiety swept through Katrina's stomach as Matthew swept her off her feet and lifted her into the wicker gondola. The moment was surreal as the basket slowly ascended into the early morning air. Never in her wildest dreams had Katrina imagined herself hot-air ballooning in France, of all places. Below them, other balloons were slowly starting to float up into the air. Brilliant colors dotted the ground below them. It was a spectacular sight.

The pilot was engaging as he explained everything that needed to be done as he guided the balloon over the expanse below. They were floating majestically and effortlessly over châteaus, medieval villages and the picturesque countryside of rural France. Behind them the sun was slowly filling the early morning sky, full and bright against the royal-blue backdrop. The morning breeze was gentle, feeling to Katrina like a brush of angel wings across her cheeks. She thought of her son and her family and Matthew, and she felt overwhelmingly blessed. Tears misted her eyes ever so slightly as she turned in Matthew's arms, reaching to kiss his lips.

"Thank you," she whispered. "This is an absolutely beautiful way to start the day."

Matthew hugged her tightly and kissed her back, allowing his lips to linger against hers. When he pulled back, he stared straight into her eyes. "You never answered my question, Katrina," Matthew whispered into the early morning air.

"What question was that?"

"Do you think you could fall in love with me, Katrina Broomes?"

There was a pause of silence, swelling between them like a too-full balloon about to explode.

"No," Katrina said finally, turning an about-face in his arms to stare back over the landscape. She leaned her back against his broad chest, pulling his arms tightly around her petite frame. She clasped both of his hands between her own and pressed her cheek to the backs of his fingers. Lifting her gaze upward, she met his stunned stare. She smiled ever so sweetly.

"No, Matthew. I don't think I can fall in love with you. I can't, because I'm already in love with you. I love you. I love you so very, very much. Without a doubt, I cannot fall into something that already has me captured heart and soul," she declared nonchalantly. Her gaze settled on the top of a cathedral in the distance, the architecture solid and exquisite. She pointed her index finger in its direction, wanting to draw Matthew's attention to it.

Shaking his head, Matthew grinned widely. He spun her

back around to face him. He drew his right palm to his chest. "Girl, you just about gave me a heart attack," he said, his head waving from side to side. "You said no, and I was just about to pass out from the devastation. What would you have done if I'd fallen out of this thing all brokenhearted?"

Katrina laughed warmly, her gazed locked with his. Matthew cupped her face in his hands, leaning to kiss her lips. It was the sweetest connection, like the gentle flutter of those angel wings beating in their hearts. Matthew dropped his forehead against hers and closed his eyes.

"I love you, too," he said, drawing back slightly so that he could linger in her stare. His eyes skated back and forth over her features, taking in every minute detail. "And I have never said that to anyone else before." A single tear misted the corner of his eye. "I love you more than you can imagine, my darling. You have become my entire world, and I don't want to ever be apart from you. God, woman, I love you!" he exclaimed, kissing her excitedly.

When the hot air balloon finally landed, their early morning ride ending with a decadent breakfast of champagne, strawberries and freshly baked croissants, Matthew was still holding tight to Katrina, their love for each other shimmering like gold between them.

At the entrance to the hotel, Matthew suddenly swept her off her feet, lifting her into his arms. Katrina's eyes widened in surprise as he carried her through the hotel lobby and into one of the waiting elevators. As the elevator door hid them from prying eyes, he kissed her boldly. He kissed her and marveled at the sheer beauty of it.

With her arms wrapped around his neck, Katrina kissed him back, desire rising like the morning mist. She could feel that everything between them had changed, becoming stronger, fuller, more intense, and she was enthralled by the magnitude of it all. It was a new day, and a new start, and together they could only just begin to imagine the possibilities.

Chapter 18

Katrina was anxious to be done with court, but the prosecuting attorney was dragging out his summation. In the back of the courtroom, Matthew had locked his stare on her, completely oblivious to the case that was playing out in the courtroom. She struggled to avoid his eyes, not wanting to draw any attention to the fact that she was more focused on Matthew, and the words he'd whispered into her ear before the session started, than on the case at hand.

She shook her head from side to side and took a deep breath. It had been three weeks since they'd returned from Paris. They'd spent the past twenty days negotiating how to navigate their relationship. Matthew was ready for them to commit, wanting her and Collin to move in with him. Katrina wasn't ready to push Collin, her son clearly not amenable to her and Matthew being in a relationship. In fact, the boy had become even more rude and ill-tempered than before, making it quite clear that he had no want of a stepdaddy. Her home had become battleground central for his teenage angst, and she wasn't ready to put Matthew through the tribulations of that.

She glanced up to see Matthew still staring at her, a smug expression painted across his face. A wave of heat spiked from the core of her feminine quadrant, and she pressed her knees together to still the urgent wanting. Matthew had called her early that morning, his tone teasing. He'd promised that he would be there to watch her in action, and he'd shown up just as promised. Behind the locked door of her office, Matthew had kissed her passionately, leaving her weak in the knees and wanting more. Before she knew it, she'd been stripped out of her clothes, her plaid skirt and white blouse draped meticulously over the leather upholstered chair. As she sat on the edge of the mahogany desk, her legs parted just so, Matthew had teased and taunted her femininity, his fingers stroking that sweet spot between her legs as he nuzzled delicate kisses against her neck.

She'd been a penny shy of unzipping his pants and releasing him from his shorts when the court clerk knocked on the door to announce that court was in session. The interruption had thrown her completely for a loop, and it had been compounded by Matthew pausing to whisper in her ear that he couldn't wait "to taste her."

There had been no time for her to re-dress, and now she sat in her judicial robe, with nothing on beneath it but a red G-string, lace-topped stockings and her conservative black pumps. Matthew knew it, and his stare indicated he fully intended to take advantage of such the moment court was concluded. Katrina's eyes widened as he pushed his tongue past the line of his full lips and licked them slowly, the gesture deliberate and teasing.

"The prosecution rests, Your Honor!"

Katrina nodded, her mind shifting from her dazed thoughts back to the suited attorney standing before her. "Thank you,

Counselor." She turned to the defense table. "Mr. Hayward, are you and your client ready to present your defense?"

"Yes, Your Honor. We are."

"Then I suggest we take a short recess and break for lunch. We will resume in one hour with your first witness," she said as she came to her feet.

"All rise!"

By the time she'd stopped by her clerk's desk to pass him her files and wish him a good afternoon meal, Matthew had made his way back to her chambers. She'd barely gotten the door locked behind them before he swept her into his arms, his lips meeting hers in a fervent kiss.

When they came up for air, Katrina laughed heartily. "You are not funny, Mr. Stallion. Not one little bit."

Matthew laughed with her. "I really wasn't trying to be," he said, "but your reaction has been priceless."

"I'd have been able to get my clothes back on if you hadn't tossed them into the closet and opened the office door."

Grinning like a cat with a mouthful of canary, he said, "I know. I didn't want you to put them back on. Do you know how sexy it is knowing that you are practically buck naked under that robe, Judge? I've been hard just thinking about it," he said, his seductive voice dropping an octave.

Katrina smiled smugly, her hand dropping to the front of his pants. "I just bet," she said, squeezing him boldly. "But I'm supposed to be working, and you are seriously distracting me!"

"Mmmm," Matthew hummed. "Yes, but you know you want to take the risk. Go on, girl! Be a little bad!" he said, leaning forward to whisper into her ear, his hands pressed against her shoulders.

Katrina placed a hand against Matthew's chest and pushed him down on the cushioned sofa. His smile was wide as he sat back, Katrina pushing his legs open with her own as she dropped down to her knees between his. He felt a twitch in the basket of his pants, jets of heat coursing through his bloodstream. His gaze locked with hers as she slowly undid the clasp to his belt and drew down his zipper.

Katrina slipped a warm hand into his pants, boldly clasping his erection in her palm. He was rock hard, his pulse throbbing in the taut muscle. A gentle groan eased past his lips as Matthew tossed his head back, his eyes shut tight. He lifted his hips to allow Katrina to pull his pants from his buttocks and down his thighs. She pushed the wealth of fabric to the floor around his feet.

His manhood waved free, eager for attention. The appendage was a rod of solid steel. His expression was coy and taunting, his eyes simmering with desire. When Katrina lowered her lips to him, sucking him in slowly, he felt as if he were ready to bust from the inside out.

Matthew felt himself becoming more and more heated beneath Katrina's ministrations. It was the sweetest sensation as she milked him gently, intent on bringing him to climax. Both marveled at how she worked him until he swelled even fuller. He moaned and made a grunt of pleasure as he spread his legs wider, allowing her full access to every square inch of his manhood.

Matthew was nearing a point of no return when Katrina sheathed him with a condom, then lifted herself from the floor, turned around and backed herself up against him. She tossed an alluring glance over her shoulder, meeting his gaze. As he grabbed her hips and ground his pelvis against the cushion of her ass, his breath caught deep in his broad chest.

Centering herself in position, Katrina gripped him tightly as she lowered herself slowly down onto his shaft. Intense ecstasy rippled through them both as Katrina rode him steadily, bouncing up and down against him. She gripped his upper thighs tightly, her body pulling and pushing him as she rode herself into a state of unrivaled bliss. Beneath her Matthew was pumping himself in and out of her, his hands clutching her hips and waist. He was enjoying the moment immensely, Katrina on him like a rodeo cowboy, and then she dropped herself down hard, her inner walls like a vise around him. The sensation was overwhelming, and all he could think of was how much he wanted to plow deeply into her.

Unable to take much more, Matthew wrapped one arm around her waist and the other around her torso. He lifted himself and her up, rolling her onto her back and down on the sofa's cushion. He planted himself firmly back inside of her, then clutched her hips as he pulled himself backward and shoved himself back in. Katrina moaned with pleasure, a look of pure delight on her face, as he stroked harder and faster. And then he exploded, spilling himself deep inside of her, fighting not to scream out loud as they both erupted in orgasm.

It had felt like forever before the couple both stopped panting heavily, gasping for cool air to stall the swell of heat that had consumed them. Sweat beaded across Matthew's brow, and a line of perspiration trickled between Katrina's breasts. When she was breathing normally, she reached for Matthew's wrist and the diamond-encrusted watch that adorned it. Making note of the time, she shook her head from side to side. She had all of fifteen minutes to regain some semblance of decency before she had to return to the judicial bench, and Matthew wasn't making that easy with the way they were wrapped so warmly around each other. He hugged her tightly as he pressed a damp kiss to the side of her face.

"I have to wash up and get back to work," Katrina said, untangling her limbs from his and moving into the bathroom that adjoined her office.

"Wouldn't you rather stay right here?" Matthew asked, leaning up on his arms, his naked body stretched across the length of the upholstery.

Inside the bathroom Katrina giggled, the running water

muffling her words. "Can you imagine the scandal? I'm sure after they called a mistrial, someone would insist on my disbarment, while you'd be able to run right on down to the country club and gloat to all the boys, who would be slapping you on the back and congratulating you on your conquest."

"I wouldn't gloat."

Katrina poked her head out, laughing heartily. "Sure you wouldn't!"

Matthew laughed with her. "What kind of man do you take me for, Your Honor?"

"A man who can get away with getting a little afternoon delight, with no one batting an eyelash at him for doing so."

"And you can't?"

"Not without folks looking at me funny."

Matthew moved into the bathroom and stood beside her, wrapping his arms around her waist and kissing the back of her neck. "Well, I'd have to argue against that theory, Judge. 'Cause you just got yourself some really, really good afternoon delight and I have no doubts that you're going to be sitting up on that bench just gloating all over the place this afternoon."

Katrina leaned back against his chest, pondering their reflection in the mirror above the small sink. She smiled, a broad grin spreading across her face, and then she laughed out loud, self-satisfaction washing over her spirit.

The evening ride was uneventful. Katrina navigated her car from the courthouse to her home the way she did every other day of the week. But today she was feeling different. She couldn't wipe the smile off her face, the Cheshire-cat grin giving away every hint of a secret that she might have wanted to keep hidden.

Matthew had been right. She'd sat through the entire afternoon court session wallowing in the sheer joy of her good time with the man. It had been a challenge to keep the smirk off her face, and both the defense attorney and the state's prosecutor had eyed her strangely more than once. She'd been too pleased when it was time to conclude, opting to recess for the afternoon and resume testimony the following day. And now she was headed home, content and satisfied, nothing and no one able to ruin her good mood.

Matthew had left her a dozen text messages throughout the afternoon, little notes professing his love and adoration for her. They had left her giggly, riding an emotional high, and Katrina couldn't imagine feeling any giddier. And then she pulled her car into her driveway to find his car already parked in front of her garage. If it had been possible, her grin would have widened even further.

Matthew hadn't said anything about meeting her. She couldn't begin to imagine what he was doing there. She glanced up to Collin's bedroom window. There was no light coming from inside. She'd spoken to the boy earlier, as he was heading to the ranch to fulfill his obligation. He'd been ecstatic about riding the horses and hanging out at the stables. No one had called to say anything was wrong, and she didn't want to imagine any antic her son might have tried causing any problems.

Letting herself inside, she called out warily. "Hello? Collin? Matthew?"

Matthew poked his head out of her kitchen. "Hey, beautiful. It's just me. Collin is at the ranch with the family. He's going to watch the football game with my brothers. I borrowed his key to let myself in. I hope you don't mind." He smiled broadly as he moved to her side, swiping his hands against a kitchen towel. He leaned forward to kiss her lips.

"No, I don't mind at all," Katrina responded, still taken by surprise.

Matthew smiled at her sweetly. "Dinner is almost ready. Why don't you go upstairs and change into something comfortable. By the time you come back down, the food should be ready to eat."

She eyed him with surprise. "You cooked? I didn't know you could cook."

He laughed. "Why do you say that like you're surprised?"

She shrugged her shoulders. "I really don't know," she said with a soft giggle. "I just am."

He kissed her again. "Well, hurry back. We're eating my famous linguine and clam sauce."

Katrina purred. "Mmm… That sounds good."

Matthew tapped her on her backside and pointed her in the direction of the stairs. "It tastes great. Now, hurry back while I put the garlic toast in the oven."

Katrina stood staring after him as Matthew moved back into her kitchen, disappearing from view. A warm smile blessed her face. She liked having a man to come home to. She'd never realized just how much. Moving up the stairs to her bedroom, she dropped down against the mattress, kicking off her high-heeled shoes. Thoughts of Matthew downstairs, puttering around in her kitchen, warmed her spirit. She felt full and content, and she found herself wanting it to last forever.

Minutes later she had tossed on a pair of sweatpants and a tank top and had pulled her hair back into a casual ponytail. Downstairs the sweet aroma of comfort food tantalized her senses. Matthew had set her dining-room table for two, her best china and crystal adorning the tabletop. Two pillar candles burned softly, and a low arrangement of fresh flowers complemented the decor.

"This is beautiful," she said as he pulled out a chair and gestured for her to take a seat. "Spectacularly beautiful," she added for emphasis.

"I'm glad you're pleased," Matthew answered with a soft smile. He moved back to the kitchen and returned swiftly with two platters of food in his hands. As Katrina watched, he used a pair of tongs to dish up plates of salad for their first course.

"Bon appétit!" he said.

Taking the first bite, Katrina realized she was hungry, not having had anything to eat since her cup of coffee and two slices of buttered toast that morning. Lunch had proven to be nourishment of a sensual kind, so as she took a forkful of baby spinach and romaine lettuce with a mix of cranberries, mandarin oranges, sweetened almonds and feta cheese, she was suddenly famished.

"Oh, my gosh, this is good!" she gushed after savoring the medley of flavors with the light balsamic vinaigrette.

Matthew grinned. "You keep saying that like you expected it to be bad! Woman, I told you I could cook."

The rest of the meal proved him true to his word as Katrina savored the linguine with its creamy sauce of garlic, mushrooms and clams.

"So how was your day?" Katrina asked as she sat back in her chair, her stomach full. She took a sip of the white wine in her crystal glass.

Matthew was savoring his own drink. "Actually it was quite productive. We had a great staff meeting this morning. And I spent the afternoon at the ranch, working with the kids. And you know what I did for lunch," he said, his eyebrows raised.

Katrina laughed. "Yes, I do."

"So, how about your day? Did you convict or not?"

"I'm still taking testimony. We reconvene in the morning."

"Maybe I should stop by to observe—"

"Maybe not," Katrina interrupted.

Matthew eyed her teasingly. "No more afternoon delight?"

"Not when I'm in the middle of a trial. It's not very professional."

Matthew snapped his fingers. "Shucks!"

The couple burst out laughing together.

"So what's for dessert?" Katrina asked.

"Woman, didn't you get enough food? That's some appetite you have."

"Don't you worry about my appetite. You can't tease me with a great meal and not give me any dessert. You just can't do it," Katrina said with a shrug of her shoulders.

Matthew's head waved from side to side. He rose from his seat, extending his hand in Katrina's direction. "Come on, then. You need to help."

As he slipped his fingers between hers, Katrina let him lead her back to the kitchen. She leaned across the center island as she watched him pull a frying pan from her cabinet. Setting it on the stove, he tossed in cherries, a pat of butter and a half cup of brown sugar and began to heat the mixture over the gas burner.

"So, how do I help?" she asked as he slowly stirred the fruit mixture.

"Fill two large glasses with vanilla ice cream," Matthew said, pointing at the refrigerator.

Following his instructions, Katrina grabbed a new container of Breyers ice cream from her freezer. When she was finished filling two oversize goblets, she stood with one hand on her hip, waiting for Matthew's next instructions.

"Do you have any brandy?" he asked, one eyebrow raised.

Katrina smiled as she reached into the upper cabinet where she stored her alcohol.

"Brandy, sir!" she said, passing him an unopened bottle of Hennessy.

Matthew cut his eye from the bottle to her and back again as he popped open the cap. Katrina laughed as he tossed her a playful look.

"It pays to be prepared," she said, giggling heartily.

Matthew rolled his eyes. "If you say so," he said with a deep laugh. After topping the cherry mixture with a splash of brandy, Matthew poured the decadent sauce on top of the ice cream.

As they settled themselves down onto the cushioned stools she kept at the kitchen counter, he lit a matchstick and placed it along the edge of the two glasses. Katrina's eyes widened with delight as a low flame burst forth from the top of each dessert. A wide smile filled her face, amusement shimmering in her eyes.

"That's some trick!" she exclaimed as Matthew bowed ever so slightly.

"Woman, I've got all kinds of tricks up my sleeves," he said cheerily.

She met his gaze with one of her own and smiled brightly. His raised eyebrows and coy smile moved her to chortle heartily.

"Make a wish," Matthew said, taking her hand in his. He gestured to the still-burning flame on her dessert as if it were a candle on a birthday cake.

She opened her mouth to be contrary, but Matthew pressed his index finger to her lips.

"Humor me," he said, reading her mind. "Just make a wish."

Closing her eyes, Katrina imagined the one thing she wanted most in the world—a lifetime with Matthew Stallion. When she had whispered her prayer skyward, she opened her eyes and leaned forward, blowing out the spark of light atop her dessert.

Matthew then blew out the flame on his own cherry-vanilla dessert. Dipping his spoon into the concoction, he scooped out a mouthful for Katrina to try. He smiled as she savored the sweet flavors, the pleasure of it washing over her expression.

"That's good!" she exclaimed as she took another spoonful.

Matthew nodded his head knowingly. "So, what did you

wish for?" he asked as he consumed his own mouthful of sweetness. He eyed her curiously.

Katrina laughed, her head waving from side to side. "Nunny!"

"Nunny?"

"Nunny yo' business!"

The man laughed heartily. "No fair. I did dinner and dessert, and you won't at least give me a hint about your wish?"

"Nope!" Katrina was scraping the last remnants of ice cream from her goblet as she cut her eye at him.

"Why not?"

She lifted herself from her seat and reached for his empty glass, intending to transport the dirty dishes from the counter to the dishwasher. She paused to plant a sticky kiss against his cheek. "Because I want my wish to come true," she answered.

Matthew wrapped his arms around her waist and drew her to him. He kissed her fervidly, his cherry-flavored lips dancing a tango against hers. As he drew back, he nodded. "I wished for the same thing," he said breathlessly.

Katrina took a deep breath, filling her lungs with air. "And what was that?" she asked, panting, his smug expression melding with her own.

"You and me forever, baby! You and me forever!"

Katrina grinned as she leaned in to kiss the flavor from his lips. "So, why don't we head upstairs," she whispered seductively. "I'm still hungry for some more dessert."

Chapter 19

Matthew's need for Katrina went bone deep. He felt it in every fiber of his being, the hunger so intense that he felt like he was starving for something he couldn't get enough of. She'd become his addiction, and he craved her with every inch of his body.

She was sleeping soundly against him. Her buttocks were curled tight against his crotch, the hard muscles of his chest pressed against her back. His arms were wrapped around her waist, and her hand rested along his hip.

He knew he needed to get up and be gone before the sunrise graced them with a new day. It had taken some finagling to convince her to let him spend the night. Mark and Michelle had agreed to keep Collin, who was excited at the prospect of an overnight at the race track. Katrina had been hesitant at first, having never considered allowing any man to spend the night in her home. That had never been the impression she wanted her son to have of her. Once plans had been made for Collin, Katrina trusting that he was safe and secure, Matthew had broken down her reluctance with his first kiss, his mouth taking possession of hers. When she'd parted her lips, he'd taken full advantage, his tongue dancing inside her mouth with unrivaled skill.

Katrina had swooned, falling deep into the seduction of it, and then she'd felt his touch, his hands sliding between her legs to gently stroke the sweetest spot. She had felt like putty beneath his touch, the intrusion so delectable that she couldn't begin to focus on anything besides his hands stroking and teasing her feminine spirit.

The sexual tension between them had stirred something deep in Matthew's core. His erection had lengthened beyond recognition, the blood throbbing like fire through his veins. His skin had prickled, conducting an electrical current from one end of his body to the other. All his senses had been heightened, and he had wanted nothing more than to fill her body with his so that they became one with each other. His satisfaction had been surpassed only by Katrina screaming his name in ecstasy as they climaxed together. They had both come together three times before midnight, and at midnight he had curled his body around hers and had fallen asleep.

The first shimmer of sunlight had moved him to open his eyes. When he did, he'd taken in his surroundings, noting that Katrina had great taste in decor. Her bedroom was simplistic, the furnishings in cool shades of tan and green reflecting her conservative demeanor. He couldn't help but wonder how she might decorate a space that was both of theirs and not just hers alone.

Thinking it made him realize just how much he wanted it. Katrina had become not only his lover but also his best friend, his confidante and his companion. He wanted her with him full-time, all the time and the more he thought about it, the more he wanted to make that happen as soon as it was physically possible.

He shifted his body closer to hers. As he did Katrina snuggled herself against him. A smile crept over her face as she awakened, and she slowly opened her eyes, tilting her head to squint up at him. The image of her resting against the pillow, her hair splayed around her head, the sweetest smile pulling at her lips and her naked body glowing from the heat in the room, aroused his senses, and he was hard as steel without even thinking about it. Katrina's smile broadened.

"So," she whispered softly, turning to face him. "Are you happy to see me, or are you *really* happy to see me?" she said with a soft chuckle as she wrapped a hand around his manhood.

Matthew laughed warmly. As Katrina stroked him slowly, he closed his eyes and took a deep breath, filling his lungs with air. The woman's touch was intoxicating, and he found himself suddenly drunk with wanting. Katrina wrapped her other arm around his shoulders as he rolled her onto her back and himself on top of her. Matthew reached for a condom from the box that rested on the nightstand. Anticipation had him about to explode as he sheathed himself quickly.

Katrina was wet and in want herself when he entered her. Her body molded itself around his hardened form, the soft lining of her inner walls kissing the length of him. She met him stroke for stroke as he pushed and pulled himself in and out of her. Their passionate lovemaking had them both panting heavily, gasping for breath. She whispered his name over and over again, and then they both exploded, Matthew spilling himself deep within.

Dropping his weight against her, Matthew nuzzled his face into her neck, drawing a trail of kisses against her jawline. As he rolled his body off her, sweat ran across his brow and down his chest. He reached for her hand and held it, entwining her fingers between his.

"I love you, Katrina," he whispered softly, his eyes shut tight.

Katrina rolled herself against him, tossing her leg over his. "I love you, too, Matthew."

Rolling onto his side, Matthew opened his eyes to stare down at her. "Marry me," he said, drawing his fingers down the length of her arm, his gazed locked with hers. "Be my wife."

Katrina's eyes widened in surprise, the question unexpected. She opened her mouth to speak and then closed it, sputtering like a fish caught out of water.

Matthew laughed. "It's a yes-or-no answer, Judge. Will you marry me?"

Laughing with him, Katrina shifted forward until her body was tight to his. She drew her palm along the curve of his cheek, her fingers dancing over his profile. "Yes," she responded, joy glistening in her stare. "Yes, I will marry you!"

Vanessa was sleeping soundly on Matthew's office sofa when he returned from a morning meeting with his brothers. Her shoes had been kicked off in a corner; her blazer tossed across the low coffee table. She lay curled in a fetal position, her arms cradling her swollen belly. Staring down at her, Matthew mused that she looked quite angelic lying there, not a care in the world reflected on her serene face.

A slight smile pulled at the corners of her mouth as he drew his hand against the line of her profile, brushing strands of hair from her face. The pad of his thumb gently brushed her cheek, and she stirred just slightly, drawing herself into a tighter ball.

With everything Vanessa had going on, Matthew worried about her. Although he knew that if any woman was capable of taking care of herself, it was Vanessa, he sensed that her nontraditional path to motherhood had been more taxing on her than she was willing to let on. Vanessa had always been like the little sister he and his brothers had never had, and so he worried about her. Even though she and her baby were not his responsibility, he felt responsible, wanting to ensure that everything went well for her and her baby.

Tiptoeing around her, he moved to his desk and took a seat in his leather executive's chair. His gaze was still focused on his friend's very pregnant form. A few times when Katrina had come to his office, she and Vanessa had passed each other in the reception area. He'd heard Katrina comment on Vanessa's progressing pregnancy once, wishing her well. Katrina had later remarked how striking Vanessa was, her pregnancy glow illuminating everything around her. He should have taken that opportunity to introduce the two women, but he hadn't.

He knew there were some who still assumed he'd fathered Vanessa's baby, and for whatever reasons he hadn't wanted that erroneous assumption to cloud what was developing between him and Katrina. With his womanizing reputation and Vanessa fanning the baby-daddy rumors, he hadn't wanted to give Katrina any reason to doubt his integrity or his intentions. He knew the two women would meet each other soon enough, and he hoped that when that happened, they would all be able to laugh off Vanessa's baby-daddy fantasy. Especially since Katrina had agreed to be his wife.

Matthew heaved a deep sigh. Across the room Vanessa rolled onto her back, her stomach bulging skyward. She rubbed at her eyes with closed fists, then struggled to sit upright. She met Matthew's gaze and smiled brightly.

"Hey, you!"

"Hey, yourself. Do you feel better?" he replied.

"I am feeling much better. How are you doing?"

Matthew nodded and returned her bright smile. "I am doing very well, all things considered."

"The judge must be treating you well!"

He laughed heartily. "The judge and I are doing just fine, thank you very much."

"I'm just checking. I heard you two had a good time in Paris."

"You didn't hear any such thing, Vanessa. You're fishing for information."

She laughed with him. "Yes, I am. So what about it? Are you going to give me any details?"

Matthew shook his head from side to side. "No, ma'am."

Vanessa rolled her eyes skyward. "I don't know why you have to be so disagreeable, Matthew. It's not like I can't find out if I really want to. Besides, you know you want to tell me."

"There is nothing for you to find out, Vanessa. Katrina and I traveled abroad and we came home. Neither of us had any complaints with our trip, and no, we didn't take any pictures that we're interested in sharing with you."

"Ohhh," Vanessa purred. "So, it was *that* kind of trip!"

"Do you ever quit, woman?"

She laughed again. "Only after I get what I want, good buddy."

"Well, there is nothing else for you to get out of me, so let it go, please."

Vanessa rose from her seat, a hand resting against her belly. She sucked in air, her eyes widening sharply. Matthew eyed her nervously.

"You okay?" he asked, concern rising in his tone.

Smiling, Vanessa nodded her head. "In another few weeks or so I will be perfect. But until then, do you think you can give me a ride over to the courthouse? I need to file some papers before they close, and I don't have the energy to drive myself."

Matthew took a quick glance at his wristwatch. "I think I can make that happen." He rose from his seat, closing the open manila folder that rested in front of him. "Come on. Maybe while we're riding, I'll tell you about my trip to Paris."

Vanessa laughed. "See, I told you I can be very persuasive!"

* * *

Katrina was laughing heartily with Maxine Bright and Nettie Banks, the two older women regaling her with their courtroom antics. It wasn't often that Katrina found her way to the county clerk's office, but the few times that she did, she enjoyed the easy banter between herself and the two women, and the two women and everybody else.

"He 'bout wet his pants when he found out you were hearing his case," Mrs. Banks said with a deep chortle. "I have never seen a man look so scared!"

Mrs. Bright laughed with her, tears misting the corners of her eyes. "I told him… I told him…" She gasped for breath before she could finish her statement. "I told him, 'Judge Broomes don't bite, baby! At least not on Wednesdays!'"

Katrina laughed, swiping at her own eyes. "You two shouldn't tease the new attorneys like that."

"We have to break 'em in right, or they aren't any good at all," Mrs. Banks teased. She rose from her seat, finished with the documents that Katrina had brought for her signature and stamp. She tapped the back of Katrina's hand as she passed the mountain of paperwork in her direction. "A little scaring is good for them. Keeps them on their toes," she said matter-of-factly.

Katrina nodded. "Well, thank you. And thank you for your help. As always I've had a very good time!"

As Katrina turned to leave, she shifted her gaze to the large window out of which both of the older women had turned to stare.

"Well, look at that!" Mrs. Bright exclaimed, crossing her arms over her chest.

"I told you the two of them would have to come out in the open sooner than later," Mrs. Banks stated, her gray head bobbing up and down with enthusiasm.

"Who's that?" Katrina asked, curious.

"Matthew Stallion," Mrs. Banks stated.

At the mention of his name Katrina's smile widened into a full grin. Excitement danced in her eyes. She felt as if she would combust with excitement, her future husband stirring a wealth of energy inside of her. She looked to where Matthew had parked his car and was getting out. As she did, the old women continued.

"And the woman with him is Vanessa Long. He's her baby's daddy," Mrs. Banks revealed.

"At least that's what they say," Mrs. Bright chimed in. "They also used to say that she didn't like men. That she had a little too much sugar in her engine, if you know what I mean," she said with raised eyebrows.

"Well, she certainly must have liked one man at least one time to be in the condition that she's in," Mrs. Banks interjected.

The two women chuckled heartily, still staring at the outside world.

Katrina recognized the woman who was getting out of Matthew's car out in the parking lot. She had seen her before, outside Matthew's office, chatting with Matthew's secretary. She watched Matthew offer his assistance, hurrying to the passenger side of the vehicle. He extended an eager hand to help her out. The two were laughing warmly together.

A flush of heat suddenly washed over Katrina's spirit. She inhaled swiftly. Confusion and jealousy tore a rift through her heart as she tried to make sense of it all. Had Matthew not been honest with her? Was he about to be a father? And what was his relationship with that woman?

"Not that we're ones to gossip," Mrs. Banks was saying, "but I'm not surprised. I came right out and asked him, and he didn't deny it. Just gave me one of his wicked smiles and winked an eye at me." She did a bad imitation, winking and grinning, grinning and winking in demonstration.

"And they're always together," Mrs. Bright added as she

laughed at her friend. "I would have thought they'd have gotten married first, though."

Her friend scowled. "Honey, hush! Young people don't worry about getting married anymore. These young girls don't think twice about having babies without a husband."

"My daughters better think about being married first. My mama didn't play like that, and neither do I!"

Mrs. Banks laughed. "You are so old-school!"

"Tch!" Mrs. Bright sucked her teeth. "And proud of it."

Katrina ignored the banter between them, still focused on what she was seeing outside the window. Matthew had wrapped an arm around the woman's shoulder, his other hand falling against her swollen belly. The two looked quite comfortable with each other. There was no mistaking the looks of adoration the woman named Vanessa was giving him, or Matthew's concerned posture as he lovingly caressed the protrusion of baby.

Katrina dropped her gaze to the floor, her eyes flitting back and forth over the linoleum floor. Nothing she had just witnessed was making any sense to her. Not one thing the two women were gossiping about seemed rational. How could the man she was head over heels in love with be having a baby with someone and she not know it? And why would Matthew not have been honest about such a thing if there were any truth to it? She couldn't begin to fathom what was going on or rationalize any of his behavior.

Glancing back up, she saw that Matthew was still in the parking lot, standing in conversation with another attorney. His pregnant friend had disappeared from view. The room suddenly felt claustrophobic. Katrina could feel tears beginning to well in her eyes, and all she wanted was to get as far from the clerk's office, and from him, as she possibly could.

Just as she was willing her body to move, the door behind her swung open and Vanessa stepped into the room. Katrina took a swift inhale of air. She shrank behind the door, hovering against the wall, wanting to disappear from sight. Vanessa's attention was focused on Mrs. Banks, the older woman chatting her up. Katrina was grateful for the diversion, praying that Vanessa didn't turn around and that Matthew stayed out in the parking lot. She didn't want to be seen, and she didn't want a confrontation of any kind until she could gain a semblance of understanding about the situation. Like a fly on the wall, she stood perfectly still, eavesdropping on the chatter around her.

"You look like you're ready to drop that baby!" Mrs. Bright chimed.

Vanessa grinned, her head bobbing up and down. "Way past ready! Junior here is making mush of my insides," she said excitedly.

The two older women laughed.

"You done dropped down low since the last time you were here," Mrs. Banks observed. "I imagine that it won't be too much longer. You and Mr. Stallion must be very excited," she said.

Vanessa nodded, grinning brightly. "We were just talking about baby names, actually."

"Do you know if it's a boy or a girl?" one of the women asked.

"No, ma'am. Not yet. I'm hoping for a boy, though. I hate to think I've been calling this kid Junior for nine whole months and it turns out to be a girl," Vanessa replied. "And Matthew was just joking that if it's a girl, we should name her Matt-lena or Matthew-anna." Vanessa's head waved from side to side. "But that's not happening!" she said with a soft chuckle.

Katrina glanced out the window. She couldn't believe what she was hearing. Everything Vanessa was saying seemed to confirm what the two women had just shared with her, corroborating that Matthew Stallion was indeed the child's father.

Matthew was still outside, in deep conversation. Katrina

wanted to move, to ease her way out the door, but she knew that to do so would draw attention to her being there. She leaned farther back against the wall, willing herself to disappear into the eggshell-colored paint. She closed her eyes and fought back the tears that threatened to spill past her lashes.

"Well, boy or girl, no matter what you name it, I know it will be a beautiful baby, 'cause Mr. Stallion is one good-looking man and you two are a beautiful couple."

Vanessa laughed. "Well, thank you, but my baby will have my good looks no matter what. Matthew's good looks don't count a lick!"

"I know that's right!" Mrs. Banks exclaimed.

Vanessa waved a quick goodbye. "I'm sure I will see you two ladies next week. Take care now," she said as she eased out the door, never turning in Katrina's direction.

The two women waved after her, both moving to get a good look out the window. Katrina took a deep breath and then a second, fighting to maintain her composure as she stared where they stared.

Outside, Vanessa made her way back to Matthew's side. As she approached, he extended his arm until his fingertips touched her stomach. Vanessa said something that was apparently very funny, because he tossed his head back in glee, laughing openly. His head was waving from side to side as he shook a finger in her direction, a wide smile still blessing his handsome face.

Vanessa shrugged her shoulders, her palms facing skyward, and it appeared that Matthew was playfully admonishing her for something he found quite humorous. Together the duo made their way back to his car, and he helped her inside, leaning to help her maneuver the seat belt comfortably around her bulbous frame.

Katrina had seen more than enough when she excused herself from the room. As she bolted out the door, Mrs. Bright and Mrs. Banks both stared curiously after her. Mrs. Banks shrugged her shoulders, cutting an eye at her friend, and then both women went back to the business they were being paid for.

Once she was out in the parking lot, Katrina's lone focus was making it to her car and home. She suddenly felt numb, wanting nothing more than to crawl beneath her covers until the past few months were nothing more than a bad memory. As she fumbled with the keys to her car, she heard her name being called from across the parking lot.

"Katrina?"

Looking up, she met Matthew's intense gaze. He was clearly surprised to see her standing there.

He looked from her to the pregnant woman and back to her again, confusion painting his expression. Tears suddenly streamed down Katrina's face. She was unable to contain the hurt of the experience a moment longer.

She turned back to her car and the keys that rattled in the palm of her hand. For a quick second it looked as if Matthew intended to move toward her, but then he spun back around, his attention clearly diverted by the other woman calling out to him. Swiping at the rush of moisture that dampened her eyes, Katrina dropped down into her vehicle, turned on the ignition and made a quick exit, heading toward home.

Chapter 20

"I'll be John Brown!" Vanessa exclaimed, her breathing coming in short gasps. "No one told me anything about this." She grimaced as a wave of excruciating pain cut through her abdomen. She screamed out in pain.

"Just hold on," Matthew barked as he floored the engine of his vehicle, the tires spinning in the direction of the local hospital. As he maneuvered through traffic, he engaged the voice-activation system for his cell phone and called the ranch. Marah picked up the telephone.

"Hello?"

"Marah, hey. It's me, Matthew."

"Hey there! What's going on?"

"I am headed to the hospital with Vanessa. I think she's having the baby."

As if to reinforce his theory, Vanessa cried out again, her screams echoing in the background.

Marah laughed excitedly. "Sounds like you've got your

hands full. I'll rally the family and we will meet you two there!"

Matthew nodded into his earpiece. "Thanks, Marah, and please, hurry!" he said after a brief pause.

Minutes later Matthew was pacing the floors of the hospital, not having a clue about what was going on. He'd pulled up in front of the emergency-room doors, and two members of the medical staff had come running with a wheelchair. By the time he'd parked his car and found his way inside, they had rushed Vanessa up to labor and delivery. As he strode from one end of the lengthy corridor to the other, he was still waiting for someone to come give him an update.

He blew a gust of warm breath past his full lips. A rash of thoughts were racing through his head. He couldn't begin to fathom how a simple trip to the courthouse could have blown up on him the way it had. He pulled his hands up and over his head, clasping them together behind the back of his neck.

There was no mistaking the look on Katrina's face. Clearly, something or someone had given her the wrong impression. The moment he'd seen her, it had been obvious. Hurt had shimmered in her dark eyes, and he knew that he was somehow responsible for the pain that had lingered in her gaze.

It had been his intent to smooth things over quickly and finally introduce the two women, but before he could get to Katrina's side, to wrap his arms around her and turn the moment around, Vanessa had screamed out in pain, pleading with him to get her some help. Then Katrina was gone and he was headed here, not having a clue where it had all gone wrong.

He depressed the redial button on his cell phone. For the umpteenth time Katrina didn't answer, his call going directly to her voice mail. He could only imagine what his good friend Vanessa had said when she'd gone inside the courthouse. He knew how she joked, and he knew that she enjoyed joking when it would not serve him well. He could only wonder if she'd said something directly to Katrina or if it was something Katrina had overheard and misconstrued. Vanessa always found her little pranks funny, but this was truly no laughing matter.

Matthew spun toward the sound of voices moving in his direction. The Stallion clan had come in full force, the whole family racing toward him excitedly.

"What's happening?" Mark asked, his arm wrapped around Michelle's waist. "Has she had the baby yet?"

Matthew shook his head. "I'm still waiting to hear something."

As if on cue, Vanessa's obstetrician, Dr. Robert Hayes, appeared from behind a closed door. His expression was serious as he extended his hand in greeting.

"Mr. Stallion, good to see you again," he said, shaking hands with Matthew.

"How is she, Doc?" Matthew asked.

"Vanessa has a severe case of preeclampsia."

"What's preeclampsia?" John asked, still holding hands with his wife, Marah.

"It's a condition where high blood pressure and excess protein in the mother's urine develop late in the pregnancy. Right now Vanessa's blood pressure is sky-high and I'm concerned about the baby's oxygen levels."

"So what does that mean?" Matthew nervously asked.

"It means that we're about to deliver this baby. We're preparing her for a C-section right now."

"Isn't it too early?" Michelle asked, her own palm pressed against her pregnant belly. "I mean, Vanessa is due after me and I still have a little while to go."

"The baby's lungs are fully developed. He'll be a little small, and we may have to keep our eye on him for a while, but I don't anticipate there will be any problems."

"So Vanessa is going to be okay?" Matthew asked.

The doctor nodded. "She's going to be just fine."

* * *

"And he never said anything about this woman?"

Katrina shook her head. "No, Lacey, not one word. He never gave me any hint that there was someone else in his life, and definitely not someone having his baby."

The two women sat in Katrina's kitchen, on cushioned stools pulled up to the counter. A bottle of Jack Daniel's and two shot glasses sat between them. Lacey filled both glasses and pushed one in her best friend's direction.

"You need to talk with him."

Katrina shook her head, screwing up her face. "I don't have anything to say to that man. I should never have let myself become attached to him."

"He loves you, Katrina. And you love him. That's obvious."

"What is obvious is that he made a fool out of me. He fathered another woman's baby, and he didn't have the decency to tell me. He and that woman will be committed to each other for the next eighteen years. I can't take that lightly, Lacey. Maybe he can but if he loved me, he should have thought that was important enough to tell me about."

Lacey heaved a deep sigh. "I still think you need to talk with him, though. Communication, remember?"

Katrina lifted her eyes to stare out into space. She suddenly felt burdened, when just hours earlier she didn't have a care in the world. Now she had more questions than she did answers, but she was afraid to ask any of them. Fearful that everything she'd come to believe about her and Matthew had been a bald-faced lie. Fearful that Matthew had never loved or wanted her the way she loved and wanted him. Fearful that the man she thought she knew well enough to commit herself to was instead a complete stranger to her. Fear was fueling every ounce of doubt and confusion in her spirit.

He had looked happy with the woman. She could tell by the way she touched her belly that he was clearly comfortable with their pregnancy. If there was any truth to what his friend had said to the two older women, then they had been thinking about names for their baby. The man she was in love with and was about to marry shouldn't have been thinking about names for a baby that was half his and wasn't half hers.

Shaking the thoughts from her head, Katrina rolled her eyes skyward as she reached for the bottle of drink and poured herself another shot. "Damn communication," she spat out. "I think we're about one baby too late for that."

Matthew wasn't accustomed to being ignored. The fact that Katrina refused to answer his calls was truly starting to annoy him. What was bothering him most was her refusal to let him explain. He desperately wanted to explain, to make things well between them.

He navigated his car through downtown Dallas, headed for Katrina's home. It was almost three o'clock in the morning, but he had no intentions of either one of them going to bed angry that night. In fact, he had no intentions of either one of them starting their day on bad terms with the other. She would hear him out, whether she wanted to or not.

He heaved a deep sigh. It had been an exceptionally long day and he was exhausted. He was past ready for a good night's sleep, but he knew he couldn't rest until he held Katrina in his arms and kissed her lips. Katrina kissing him back would mean that the two of them were on track again, and he needed that more than he had ever needed anything before. He needed Katrina to love him and to trust his love for her. He needed her more than she would ever know.

Matthew pulled his car to a stop at the intersection of Skillman Street and Royal Lane. He waited for the red light to turn green, strumming his fingers impatiently against the steering wheel.

A wry smile pulled at the corners of his mouth. Just a few short hours ago, after giving birth to a five-pound-four-and-one-half-ounce baby boy, Vanessa had scolded him for not rushing after Katrina sooner. He could only shake his head at the absurdity, since all of this was her fault as far as he was concerned. Vanessa hadn't seen it his way, having no understanding of what he was being so sensitive about.

He and his brothers had been in awe of the little bundle of life that had slept so peacefully in their friend's arms. And there had been no missing that young Master Vaughan Long had his donor father's looks, the child blessed with green eyes, light brown curls and a more cream than café au lait complexion. Even Vanessa had eyed her baby boy with surprise, laughing heartily that baby Vaughan looked nothing at all like his mother and had not one single, solitary Stallion family feature.

Once Matthew had been assured that mother and child were both well, he had blasted their family friend once again for her cavalier attitude toward people thinking he had fathered her child. "The truth has surely revealed itself," Vanessa had said with a deep chuckle, and it had, as they had all joked that Matthew didn't even need a blood test to prove that Vanessa's baby wasn't his.

Pulling into Katrina's driveway, Matthew parked his car and hurried to her front door. Ringing the bell, he waited anxiously for someone to answer. Not a single light illuminated the inside. Ten minutes later he was still standing outside the spacious home, no sign of Katrina to be found.

Chapter 21

At that very moment what Katrina was most thankful for was the anonymity. She'd found a comfortable corner in the lobby of the Brisas Del Mar Inn. The space was warm and inviting with its Mediterranean decor, and there was no one there who knew her or knew anything about her. In fact, with the exception of the hotel's front desk clerk, a woman with a dark mahogany complexion and black-suede eyes, there was no one else there. Katrina imagined that all the other guests were ensconced in the inn's lavish and romantic suites, having settled down for the night.

Katrina hadn't been able to sleep, and so she had tossed on a pair of cotton sweats and had walked the immaculate property, admiring the views of the Santa Ynez Mountains off in the distance as the last remnants of sunlight settled behind the foothills. Then she'd found a lush recliner in the corner of the lobby, poured a cup of English toffee-flavored coffee and rested herself there, trying to free her mind of Matthew Stallion.

She heaved a deep sigh. It had been four weeks and she'd managed to successfully avoid any and all contact with the man. After her encounter with his friend Vanessa in the county clerk's office, she'd asked for an emergency leave of absence to tend to a personal matter. Then she'd packed her son off to his grandparents' home in Arizona for an impromptu visit. Once she was assured that Collin was safe and content, she'd secreted herself away to one of her favorite spots in Santa Barbara.

Her personal cell phone had been left behind in Dallas, the device neither missed nor wanted. It was easier not to think about calling him when she didn't have to look at her cell phone tempting her. And she didn't want to know if he was trying to call her. And now she'd found herself a comfortable corner to dwell in, relieved not to have to sit another lonely night in her lavish suite, thinking about him and the woman having his baby.

The woman having his baby. Katrina shook her head from side to side. One month ago she'd felt betrayed. She couldn't begin to comprehend why Matthew would have withheld that kind of information from her. She'd been manic, almost obsessed about it. Her reaction had thrown her for a loop. She didn't understand why she was riding an emotional roller coaster over it all, when usually she was able to take everything in stride. Then a visit to her family physician for something to calm her nerves and help her sleep had given her a secret of her own to hide.

Katrina heaved another deep sigh, her palm falling to her abdomen. The doctor's news had been a complete shock. She was still unraveled by the revelation, her mind entertaining the memory of the moment. Dr. Wallace Brandt's warm smile had been a welcome sight as he'd come into the examination room, clipboard and ink pen in hand.

"Katrina, my friend! What brings you here this morning?"
Katrina had shrugged her shoulders skyward. "Hi, Dr.

Brandt. I've been experiencing some minor anxiety and was hoping you'd be able to give me something to take the edge off."

"Have you been sleeping?"

"No, sir, not well."

"What's going on in your life, Katrina?" he'd asked as he peered into her ears with a light scope. "How's work?"

She'd shrugged again. "I was appointed to a new district. It's been challenging."

"And your personal life? What's going on there?"

There was a moment of silence as she met the doctor's inquisitive stare. The answer was painted all over her face, her emotions awhirl. Her doctor nodded his head as if she'd answered out loud, his all-knowing look moving her to roll her eyes.

Dr. Brandt chuckled. "I get the impression there's a story there," he said, pressing a stethoscope to her back.

"Nothing I'm interested in sharing," she said softly, fighting back the emotion from her tone.

The doctor nodded as he leaned back against the room's counter, eyeing her chart with interest. "I see my nurse took some blood and urine already."

"Yes, she did."

"When was your last period?" the doctor asked, lifting his eyes to meet hers.

Katrina's expression was suddenly blank. "Well…it was… no…" she muttered, her eyes darting back and forth as she tried to remember the exact date of her last menstrual cycle. "I don't…" She paused, her eyes suddenly widening.

The doctor held up his hand. "Give me a minute," he said as he moved to the door and out into the hallway.

Katrina's thoughts were on fast-forward as she tried to establish a time line that actually made some sense to her. When she failed, a wave of panic suddenly consumed her. When the doctor returned to the room, she was bent forward, her head between her legs as she gasped for air. The physician's large hand against her shoulder moved her to sit back up.

"We just ran a urinalysis, and we'll run a blood test to confirm the diagnosis, Katrina, but it would seem that you are pregnant. Congratulations!"

She was completely floored by the doctor's news. She opened her mouth to speak, then closed it just as quickly. Her heartbeat was pounding harshly in her chest. She took a deep breath, held it and blew the air past her lips.

"That's not possible," she said finally. "We used a condom. We *always* used a condom," she said emphatically.

The doctor nodded. "I'm sure you did, but condoms do have a failure rate. Even with perfect condom usage, and that means using condoms consistently and correctly every single time, three out of every one hundred women may find themselves pregnant. I have no doubts that you and your partner acted in a very responsible manner, but you have just found yourself one of a very small minority of women who experience an unintended pregnancy while on some form of birth control."

Katrina dropped her body back against the examining table. She pulled her hands to her face, covering her eyes with her fingers. She couldn't begin to fathom how any of this could have happened.

Katrina shook the memory from her thoughts. Her stomach quivered ever so slightly, a light flutter of nervous energy wafting through her spirit. She took a sip of her hot drink and shifted her body around in her seat. For the past few weeks she'd been living with the knowledge that she was pregnant with Matthew Stallion's baby, and she still didn't have a clue what she planned to do about it.

What she did know was that she couldn't hide out forever. When she'd spoken to Collin, her son had asked when they would both be heading back home to Dallas, the boy already weary of his grandparents and wanting to be back among his friends. He'd complained about everything from the dry Arizona heat to having to actually do chores around the family's home. "I'm missing school!" he'd whined, both of them knowing that it was not his classes he was anxious to get back to. The teachers had sent his schoolwork with him, and she knew that his grandfather, a stern disciplinarian, had already ensured that every ounce of it was finished. But she didn't have an answer for him, not knowing when she would be ready to face him, or Matthew, with the news that she was pregnant.

Pregnant and unmarried. This was hardly the example she wanted to set. This was so far removed from the example she should have been setting. She waved her head from side to side, drawing her knees to her chest as she dropped her forehead against them. She had always lectured her son to be responsible. She had continually told him that sex before marriage was a definite no-no, that such an intimate act should be reserved for the sanctity of a loving, committed relationship. *Commitment* being the key word. Even if she hadn't practiced what she'd been preaching, she hoped her son would never find that out.

And what about the young women she frequently mentored? What lessons was she teaching them about responsibility and parenting? Although people barely batted an eyelash at pregnancy outside marriage anymore, Katrina had been raised differently and had always wanted her actions to reflect those teachings. She wanted the young women who looked up to her to know that saving themselves was nothing to be ashamed of, and that if a man truly loved them, then not only would he be willing to wait, but he would be willing to commit to marriage before starting a family. She often lectured that getting pregnant and having a baby were no guarantee for a successful, loving relationship with any man, and she often told young women not to think that such a thing was an option.

She heaved a deep sigh. There was much they would all have to deal with, and in that moment Katrina couldn't begin to comprehend what life would be like once they returned to the real world. Everything felt beyond her control and it was not a feeling she liked. She was also still lost in her own pity party, enjoying her woes much too much. But as she took one last sip of her flavored drink, she committed to shifting back into a semblance of normalcy before the week was out.

She still had her child to care for and another on the way, and if nothing else, both of her babies needed her to be a strong example for them to emulate. Running from her problems wasn't what she wanted Collin, or the new baby, to learn. It wasn't who she was, and so she decided in that very moment that no matter what happened from that point forward, she would be the strong, dependable woman she knew herself to be. And she would be the woman having Matthew Stallion's baby.

"I need your help," Matthew stated the minute Vanessa had opened her front door.

She laughed heartily, her head waving from side to side. "Good morning to you, too!"

Baby Vaughan was cradled against her breast, suckling eagerly. His mother gestured with her index finger for Matthew to follow her inside.

"I mean it, Vanessa," Matthew said emphatically as he closed the front door behind them. "I really need your help."

"What's wrong?" Vanessa said as she moved back to the rocking chair inside her living room. She adjusted the baby against her lap. "What's got you so twisted?"

Matthew moved to her kitchen and the refrigerator, reaching inside for a container of orange juice. He focused his gaze on everything but Vanessa and her nursing infant. "Are you almost finished?" he asked, pouring juice into a glass.

"Does my feeding my son make you uncomfortable?" Vanessa's smile was teasing.

Matthew waved a dismissive hand. "No. I just need your full attention. This is important."

"Your godson is important, too. My baby boy has a hearty appetite. He's also like his mother. He doesn't like to be denied. You know, I think he's going to be a breast man, too," she said, laughing.

Matthew winced as he shook his head. "I swear, woman!"

"So, what do you need?" she asked as she drew the baby to her shoulder, patting him lightly on his back so that he burped the excess air from his tummy.

"I need you to help me find Katrina."

"Where did she go?" Vanessa asked.

Matthew tossed her an annoyed look. "If I knew where she went, I wouldn't be asking you to help me find her, now, would I?"

"How do you lose your woman?"

"I had you running interference in my life. Any woman would run."

"I was just doing what I do best. Personally, I've never had a problem holding on to my women."

Matthew rolled his eyes. "Good for you, Vanessa. But now you need to fix the mess you made by helping me find my girl. Please."

"Are you sure you really want to find her? I mean…"

Matthew cleared his throat, moving to the couch and dropping down against the cushions. "Don't go there, Vanessa. I am not in the mood this morning."

His friend smirked, shaking her head. She lifted herself and her son from the rocking chair. She crossed the room and laid the infant in Matthew's lap.

"Support his head," she said as she buttoned her cotton blouse, adjusting it around her full chest. Moving to the desk on the far side of the room, she shuffled through a pile of papers, pulling one of the documents into her hands. She moved over to where Matthew sat and dropped down beside him, passing the paperwork to him. "I'm already a step ahead of you. John hired me a week ago."

Matthew cut his eye in her direction as he cooed and made faces at his godchild. "John asked you to look for Katrina?"

"He figured that by the time you got around to asking, most of the legwork could already be finished," she said, nodding. "And he was right."

"Why would my brother ask you to find Katrina?"

"Because you've been moping around like a little lost puppy since she disappeared. You don't want to admit it, but you're pissed off that she won't talk to you. Then you let your pride get in the way. If she won't talk to you, then you're not going to talk to her. Now you're missing her so badly that you can't focus on anything. Just getting all up in your own way. It didn't take rocket science to figure out that you would need a little help."

Matthew inhaled, taking a deep breath of oxygen. He wanted to protest but knew his friend was right. "So what did you find out?" he asked instead as he nuzzled the baby beneath his chin.

"I tracked her credit-card charges. She really wasn't too difficult to find."

"And you were able to do this how?"

Vanessa grinned. "Let's just say I have friends in high places," she answered with a wink of her eye.

Matthew stared at the document before him. "So this is where she is now?"

"It's where she's been for the last few weeks."

Matthew reached for Vanessa's hand and squeezed it. "Thank you."

Vanessa smiled. "Don't ever say I didn't do right by you, big daddy!"

He smiled back. "Is there anything else I need to know?"

She nodded. "The Stallion jet is already fueled and ready to take off whenever you are. John said to call him as soon as you get everything straightened out."

"And he knew I'd be going because...?"

"Because I called him right after you called me to say you were on your way over."

Matthew laughed. "I love my family."

Vanessa laughed with him as she reached for baby Vaughan. "I love our family, too! Now give me my baby and get out of here."

As the pilot announced their descent toward the Santa Barbara Municipal Airport, Matthew's stomach flipped and curdled with anxiety. Since takeoff he'd done nothing but recite over and over in his head what he planned to say to Katrina. Now that he was minutes away from being able to see her, the words were a jumbled mess in his head.

Since he last saw Katrina, he'd had much he wanted to say, starting with just how unhappy he was with her ignoring him. Matthew wasn't accustomed to any woman ignoring him so blatantly. And Katrina's disregard had been blatant. It had left him with hurt feelings, had made him mad and had him questioning whether or not he was cut out for a monogamous relationship.

Once he'd moved his ego out of the way, he'd been worried that something might have happened to her or Collin. When he'd discovered she had taken a brief leave of absence from court and had pulled her son out of school for an extended period of time, he'd gone looking for her friend and neighbor.

Lacey had been a fountain of information, spilling admonishments and accusations faster than a water pipe with a leak. She'd been protective of her best friend, and since Katrina had declared him to be lower than low, Lacey had considered him a doormat and nothing more. He was hardly surprised when Lacey told him that Katrina knew about Vanessa and the baby. He didn't bother to tell her the truth. Katrina was the only one who mattered. But Lacey hadn't given him anything to go on, refusing to tell him where he could find the woman he was in love with.

With that door slammed squarely in his face, Matthew had become even more frustrated. He'd also become even more adamant about finding Katrina and setting things straight between them. Toward that end he couldn't deny Vanessa's private-investigator skills, their family friend having proven herself to be very adept at finding a very small needle in a very large haystack. And just like he knew she would, Vanessa had come through for him.

Now here he was, landing in Santa Barbara, about to come face-to-face with Katrina, and his mind was a complete and total mush. Matthew blew a deep sigh, secured his seat belt and waited for the aircraft to touch down.

Chapter 22

Matthew had barely checked into the hotel before he was searching the property for her. After instructing the hotel's staff to deposit his luggage in his room, he had finagled her room number from the front desk clerk and had gone knocking on her door. When he'd gotten no answer, he'd gone searching the inn's lavish grounds.

He saw Katrina well before she saw him. She lay on a cushioned lounger in the hotel's lush gardens, overlooking Santa Barbara's West Beach. She wore a conservative black bathing suit that accentuated her curves and a floral print pareu wrapped around her hips. Her feet were bare, her manicured toes wiggling back and forth. She lay there deep in thought, oblivious to everything around her. He stood staring, able to exhale now that he could see that she was safe and well. She was even more beautiful than he remembered. There was a glow about her, and she looked well rested and very relaxed. Energy suddenly coursed through his bloodstream, firing every one of his nerve endings. He almost hated the thought of disturbing her peace, but he had no intentions of being so far from her for one second longer. He took a deep breath and then a second as he moved in her direction.

Katrina's mind was racing as she lay out on the lounger, enjoying the sunshine and the midday warmth. For the first time that day she wasn't nauseous, her morning meal not feeling as if it wanted to come back and haunt her. In fact, she felt amazingly calm and content. As content as she had felt before she and Matthew had fallen out with each other. It was as if a blanket of security had dropped down onto her shoulders. Every fiber in her being seemed to sense that all would be well.

A dark shadow suddenly blocked the sunlight that had been raining down on her. The intrusion disrupted her thoughts. Katrina was momentarily startled as she shaded her eyes with her hand to see who or what had gotten in her way. And then she saw him, a bright smile blessing his dark face as he stared down at her.

Katrina sat upright in her seat, her eyes widened in disbelief. "Matthew?"

"Surprise," he said, trying to keep his moderate tone void of the intense emotion that was washing like a tsunami over his spirit.

"How did you…? What are you doing here?"

Matthew inhaled swiftly, reaching the back of his hand out to stroke the side of her face. "I came to take you back home. I miss you," he said softly.

"I…I…" Katrina stammered, not sure how to respond. The warmth from his hand took her breath away, his fingers gently stroking her skin. She had never expected to see him there, in that space, and his presence suddenly had her completely discombobulated.

Matthew dropped down to his knees beside her. Against the backdrop of the bright blue ocean and light sand, he looked out of place in his tailored Italian suit, the navy blue silk fitting him like a second skin. With his bright white dress shirt and paisley tie he struck quite a figure, not one eye having missed his arrival. Katrina was equally awestruck.

He pulled both of her hands into his, drawing the backs of her fingers to his lips. "So, how do I fix this?" Matthew asked, his eyes flitting over every line and curve of her exquisite face. "How do I make everything right between us? Because none of this feels right, Katrina. Nothing in my life is right without you there."

Katrina met his intense gaze. "I don't know that we can fix this, Matthew. I would think that under the circumstances your priorities are much different now. I don't know that I fit into those priorities anymore."

"You are my *first* priority, Katrina. And you always will be. Absolutely nothing has changed. When I told you I loved you, I meant it with every fiber of my soul. I love you, and I want to spend the rest of my life with you. I asked you to marry me, and I meant that, as well. I want you to be my wife. Baby, I love you!"

Katrina waved her head from side to side. She pointed her index finger at him, wagging it at him. "Don't say that. If you truly loved me, you would have told me about your baby. You would have told me that you were about to be a father. I would have known that some other woman, who you will now have to be committed to for the next umpteen years, was having your child. Love would have been honest with me."

Matthew nodded. His tone was firm. "That's correct. And I *would* have told you. Katrina, I have never been dishonest with you. I never told you about my friend Vanessa and her baby because there was nothing for me to tell. I am *not* responsible for Vanessa's son. Vanessa is an old family friend and my *client*. Because of the legal ramifications of her pregnancy, I was bound by our attorney-client privilege to honor her privacy. But I repeat, I am *not* her baby's daddy!"

"But—"

"But nothing," Matthew interrupted. "You never gave me an opportunity to explain. You heard the rumors and you assumed the worst about me. Then you ran. And since we're laying our cards out on the table, you need to know that I didn't appreciate that. I don't appreciate the woman I love, the woman I consider to be my life partner, not communicating with me when things start to get tough. If we're together, I need to be able to trust that when we hit a wall of any kind, I can depend on you to help me knock it out of our way. I need you to trust me, and I want to be able to trust you, Katrina."

Tears rose to Katrina's eyes. "In my defense, to hear another woman say that you two were picking out names for your baby threw me off balance. I reacted with emotion, and admittedly, I may have been wrong to do so. I should have gathered my facts and then responded instead."

"You should have," Matthew said, pulling at his necktie until he'd loosened it from his neck. "If you'd had all the facts, we wouldn't be here right now."

"But why would your friend imply that you fathered her child if you hadn't?"

Matthew shook his head from side to side. "Once you meet Vanessa, you'll understand. She's a piece of work!" he exclaimed. "But I can assure you I have never been intimate with Vanessa, and it is physically impossible for me to be the father of her child."

There was a moment of silence between them as Katrina reflected on his words. She was suddenly more confused than ever. Matthew captured her hands again and caressed them between his own. Katrina lifted her eyes to meet his. She heaved a deep sigh.

"I guess I owe you an apology, Matthew. I didn't mean for this to get out of control, but I've been a little overwhelmed with things. More than you know right now. I jumped to the wrong conclusion. I'm so sorry. Can you forgive me?"

Matthew cupped her face between his palms and leaned

forward to kiss her lips. "There's nothing to forgive. I never meant for you to be hurt by any of this. I should have done a better job of reeling in Vanessa. But she's been running over me and my brothers since we were all kids. She got out of hand, and I should never have allowed it. I'm the one who should be apologizing to you."

Katrina wrapped her arms around his neck. She hugged him tightly, savoring the sensation of his large frame pressed to hers. Butterflies danced in her midsection, and if she didn't know better, she would have sworn that their baby had kicked her with glee.

Their baby. A tremor of anxiety suddenly shot through her body. She and Matthew had never discussed children before. They had never had the opportunity. Katrina didn't even know if Matthew wanted kids or not. He had been wholeheartedly accepting of Collin and wanted a family that was ready-made for him. But was he at all interested in parenting a child from infancy to adulthood? Katrina didn't know, and suddenly she was afraid to ask. It wasn't as if she had any intentions of changing her plans if he wasn't interested in participating. She bit down against her bottom lip, her expression strained.

"What's wrong, baby? You don't look happy."

Katrina met his concerned stare. She opened her mouth to answer but had second thoughts about it. She shook her head. "Nothing. I just…" She paused, letting her eyes roam over the landscape. She took another deep breath. "How's your friend doing?" Katrina asked softly.

Matthew lifted himself up from where he'd been kneeling on the ground. He pulled his arms out of his suit jacket and folded the garment neatly over the back of the lounger that rested beside hers. Pulling his necktie off, he laid it down with the jacket, then kicked off his shoes. Resting on the side of the lounger, he pulled off one black sock and then the other. Then he pulled himself up closer to her, bringing his lounger and his body as close to her as he could manage.

"Vanessa is the proud mother of a beautiful baby boy that she's named Vaughan," he finally answered.

Katrina looked surprised. "I didn't realize she was due this soon."

"She wasn't. She was actually due after my sister-in-law, but she was diagnosed with preeclampsia, so she had to have an early C-section. That day we saw you at the clerk's office, she became symptomatic and I had to rush her to the hospital. That's what kept me from catching up to you before you got away."

Katrina paused, suddenly feeling just shy of foolish for the way she'd reacted that day. "Are she and the baby doing well?" she finally asked. "There weren't any complications, were there?"

"Not a one. He's a cute little guy. The family already has him spoiled rotten. You have to see Marah, Mitch and the rest of the girls fighting over who gets to hold him. There isn't enough baby for all the outstretched arms in the house."

Katrina smiled ever so faintly, unable to stop herself from wondering what they would all think about one more little addition to the Stallion brood. She looked up to find Matthew studying her intently. She gave him the brightest smile she could muster.

"Babies bring out the best in people," she said nonchalantly.

"That they do," Matthew said in agreement. "But I don't want to talk about Vanessa. And I definitely don't want to talk about her baby. I want to talk about you and me. Us. Something doesn't feel right, Katrina, and I want to know what it is. I feel like you're holding back. So, what is it? What are you keeping from me? Because I can see that something is definitely the matter." He drew his lounger even closer to hers, pulling her legs atop his as he turned her toward him, wanting her full attention. "Baby, talk to me," he implored.

Katrina stared at the man, her stomach doing 360-degree turns. She took a deep breath, searching for the perfect words to tell him of her condition. Words failed her when Matthew dropped his hands to her waist and pulled her into his lap. Her eyes widened, the gesture unexpected. He wrapped his arms around her torso and hugged her tightly. Katrina allowed herself to sink into the warmth of the embrace. As he held her, nuzzling his face into her neck, she realized just how much she had missed him. She clutched him closer, never wanting to let him go again.

The tears she'd been fighting suddenly rained past her lashes, saline rolling over the curves of her cheeks. Matthew brushed the moisture away with the back of his hand. He leaned to kiss her forehead and then her mouth, allowing his lips to linger against the soft pillows.

"I missed you so much," he whispered, his warm breath filling her spirit. "I can't tell you how lost I felt without you."

Katrina nodded, her forehead pressed against his. "I'm sorry. I just needed some space. It was all just too much for me to handle. I know I shouldn't have left the way I did but…"

Matthew pressed his index finger to her lips. "Shhh… Don't…" He shook his head from side to side. "Baby, just remember that there is nothing that we can't handle together," Matthew said, his large hands gently caressing her back and shoulders. "I hope that I never do anything to hurt you, but I would hope that you'd trust me enough to talk to me when you're not sure about something that I have done."

He kissed her mouth again as she nodded her head. Tears were still flowing from her eyes, and he held her close as she cried quietly against him.

"I don't know why I'm so emotional," Katrina said with a soft giggle. But she did know. And she needed to tell him. She took a deep breath and held it, allowing the warm air to flood her lungs. When she blew it back out, she met his gaze.

Desire lingered in the stare, her own wanting reflected back in the look he was giving her. Whatever was between them had risen in full bloom, as if they'd never been apart from one another. Shivers of anticipation raced up her spine, and every one of her nerve endings seemed ultrasensitive. She wanted him, her need almost volatile and ready to explode. She instinctively knew he wanted her just as badly.

Rising from his lap, Katrina needed to put some distance between them. If only for a quick moment she welcomed the sliver of breeze that managed to cool the space between them. Matthew reached his hand out to her, entangling his fingers between hers.

She pulled her hand from his, clasping it close to her body. The sensations were too much; her want of him consuming. "I need to go back to my room," she muttered.

He nodded. "I'd love to keep you company," Matthew said, his expression begging for an invitation. He had come to his feet and stood staring at her, his gaze making her hot from one end of her body to the other.

She didn't need words to convey to him that he could follow her. Every fiber of her being was begging for his attention. He tossed his suit jacket and his necktie over his arm as he reached for her hand a second time. Katrina followed willingly as Matthew led her inside, heading directly for her luxury suite.

When they were behind the closed door, Matthew dropped everything to the floor and snaked his arms around her waist. He leaned over to kiss her mouth, pressing his lips to hers as if he were kissing her for the very first time. The gesture was soft and teasing as flesh glided easily against flesh. Katrina felt as if she could linger in that moment forever.

With some urgency he pushed his tongue past the line of her teeth, teasing her tongue in a slow, sensuous tango. Katrina was all aflutter from the sensations sweeping through her. Every muscle in her body quivered with excitement. She wrapped her thin arms around his neck and drew him closer, lapping hungrily at his lips. The kiss became more frenzied, and with their bodies pressed so tightly together, Katrina could feel the first stirrings of his erection.

She pulled back, panting as if she'd just run a race. She felt as if she had won and Matthew's touch was the sweetest prize. She took a deep breath and then a second, desperate to ease the intense heat that had flooded her body. "I need a shower," she said, her raspy breathing inciting him even more.

She moved in the direction of the bathroom, her steps slow and easy as she untied the silk pareu from around her waist. When she reached the entrance, she dropped it to the floor beneath her feet.

As she eased into the bathroom, Matthew followed on her heels. He leaned back against the door frame, his arms folded across his chest as he continued to watch her. She tossed him a sly smile over her shoulder. As Katrina met his gaze, she couldn't help but think that his stare was like the sweetest caress.

Knowing that he was eyeing her every move excited her. She turned her back to him and began undressing, easing the straps of her bathing suit off one shoulder and then the other. She paused to step out of her sandals before pushing the fabric of her swimsuit around her waist and down over her buttocks. She bent forward, and her bare bottom was completely exposed as she wiggled out of her suit and kicked it aside.

Matthew's smile widened. Still leaning against the door, he'd not moved an inch, but one muscle had expanded substantially, the length of his erection pressing heavily against his inner thigh. Katrina turned slowly around, her gaze meeting his evenly, then slowly dropping down the length of his torso. Matthew could feel her eyes homing in on the crotch of his pants. Deciding that it was definitely time to give her something to look at, he began to undress, as well.

His shirt came first, landing atop her silk pareu in the doorway. As he moved to where she stood, Katrina whispered his name, the lilt of it like a sweet serenade against his ears. In the few seconds that it took him to reach her side, he'd stripped completely naked, his pants and briefs landing next to her swimsuit. Her hands rested against the lean line of his waist as she stepped to him. She stood on the tips of her toes to kiss his mouth, moving her lips hungrily over his.

Her want of him was bone deep, so intrinsic to her spirit that for the first time in weeks she felt like could breathe easy again. It was as if she'd not been able to get a good breath of air since she last saw him in that parking lot. She wound her arms around his neck, her fingers against the back of his head as she kissed him harder.

Matthew marveled at how easily she fit into his arms, the limbs molded around her frame as if they'd been carved precisely for her. He drew her closer, his skin shimmering beneath her touch, revived by the simple fact of her presence. He'd missed her. He needed her, his desire so tenacious that it was reeling through his bloodstream with a vengeance.

His tongue danced inside her mouth, dueling with hers, the two of them suddenly frantic to get as close to each other as they could. Matthew wrapped his arms around her torso and lifted her against him, and Katrina locked her legs tightly around his waist. Easing into the large shower, he reached behind them and turned on the faucet.

The first spray of water was ice-cold against Katrina's back but she barely noticed, the heat rising off her body like a firestorm. Her nipples had hardened against his broad chest, the rock-hard candies teasing his senses. It was almost too much for him to bear. His erection strained between his legs, his pulse throbbing through the steely muscle, desperate for relief.

Beneath the water, which had warmed nicely as it rained down on them, Matthew pressed her back to the wall. Every coherent thought was gone from him. All he could think of was burying himself deep inside her until he was completely lost in the lust of their union. He eased his hand between them, teasing the door to her most private place. Her juices flooded his fingers, and he knew she was as anxious for him to be where he was as he was to be there.

Dropping his mouth against her neck, he nuzzled his face into the curve beneath her chin, biting lightly at the soft flesh. Katrina moaned loudly, the sweet mating call vibrating through him. He reached for his erection, stroking the length of it, and then he eased himself inside of her.

Katrina's fingers dug into his shoulders as she felt him enter, the muscles of her inner walls clenching him like a vise grip. Their connection was the sweetest union that either of them could ever imagine. Matthew's heart rate was racing as he pumped in and out of her, pounding his body against hers. His hands cradled her buttocks as he pushed and pulled her against him.

Water poured down on them, saturating their heads and cascading over their torsos. Her eyes were closed tight, lust painting her expression. Moisture blurred Matthew's vision and he closed his eyes shut, his forehead kissing hers. He felt himself drawing closer to the edge as her hips cradled his pelvis, allowing him to drive deeper into her.

Katrina suddenly threw her arms back over her head, her hands raised as she surrendered to the moment, the sweeping sensations consuming her. Matthew held her securely around the waist, her torso braced against the wall. Her lengthy legs gripped him firmly, her feet locked about his buttocks. Matthew thrust forward again and again, reclaiming every second that they had been apart. And then she screamed his name over and over again, the lilt of it rolling off her tongue as if she were in prayer.

Matthew exalted in hearing her, her throes of pleasure inciting his own. He gasped heavily, and then his body exploded with the ferocity of a volcano. As he felt himself spilling into her, Katrina clenched her muscles, milking every ounce of his desire from him. As they climaxed together, both panting heavily, Matthew fell against her, bracing his hands against the wall beside her shoulders, his body still holding up hers. Neither of them wanted to let the other go. Neither of them wanted to break the intimate connection.

Minutes later they lay sprawled across the bed, her naked body straddling his. It had taken only the mere thought of pleasuring her to make him full and hard again. His manhood had come to full attention under her ministrations, her hands caressing him softly. His blood had surged when Katrina had taken him into her mouth, wrapping her lips and tongue around him as if she were sucking a lollipop. She had teased and taunted him until he was engorged and ready to bust, and then she had dropped her body down against his and was riding him with everything she had in her.

Matthew reached for her breasts, the globes swollen, full. Her nipples were hard, and he lifted himself up to suckle one and then the other, his tongue flicking eagerly over them. Katrina arched her back, clutching him tightly. And then they both exploded, every nerve ending in their two bodies erupting in pleasure.

Matthew had lost count of the number of times she'd been able to revive his erection. Their desire for each other had been palpable, both of them so consumed with want that it felt as if they were starved and were able to feed themselves for the very first time. Katrina lay curled against him, her breathing finally light. He turned and pressed himself into her, the curve of her buttocks cradled against his crotch. Her head rested on his arm. His other arm was tossed over her abdomen, the weight of his palm resting atop her stomach.

As his fingers gently caressed her flesh, Katrina closed her eyes and took a deep breath. She inhaled once and then twice before opening her eyes again, her gaze resting on the curtained window across the room.

"Matthew?"

"Yes, my darling?"

"There's something important that I need to tell you."

Matthew pressed himself closer to her. "Honey, you should know that you can tell me anything. What is it?" he asked as he kissed the back of her neck, nuzzling her gently.

There was a brief pause as Katrina took another breath and held it. She blew warm air past her lips, her heart beating rapidly. Goose bumps rippled across her arms.

Matthew sensed her hesitancy. He lifted himself up and rolled her over onto her back to stare down at her. "What's wrong, Katrina?" he asked, concern rising in his tone.

She met his gaze and held it, his stare comforting as his eyes flickered back and forth across her face. "We're having a baby, Matthew," she said softly. "I'm pregnant with your child."

Matthew stared. Her words echoed in his ears. *Pregnant. Baby. His baby!* He was going to be a father. He sat upright, throwing his legs off the side of the bed. Katrina sat up beside him, staring intently. She was waiting for him to respond, anxiety rising in her expression. Her words echoed in his heart. The woman who had his heart was having his baby. He was going to be a father. The realization of that hit him, and until that very moment he hadn't known just how much he wanted such a thing. He reached and pulled her into his arms. He couldn't stop himself from kissing her, plastering her face and mouth with damp kisses. Excitement bubbled from his midsection as he laughed with glee.

"Sweetheart, that's wonderful!" Matthew exclaimed excitedly, hugging her tightly. "When…? How long…?" He had a million questions and didn't know where to begin.

Sensing his desire for more details, Katrina gave him as much information as she could. "I found out just before I left Dallas. I wasn't feeling well, and with everything that had happened, I just thought it was stress. I went to my doctor, hoping he would give me something, and…well…surprise. With everything that was going on with you, and believing what I believed, I thought it best for me to take some time to myself to mull it all over and try to figure out what I wanted to do."

Matthew was nodding, his gaze unwavering as he studied her intently. He pressed his fingers to her tummy, then leaned over to kiss her belly button. Resting his cheek against her stomach, he took a deep breath, trying to stall the wave of excitement that coursed like thunder through his body. Her body trembled with nervousness beneath him.

"You do want to keep this baby?" he asked suddenly. "I mean…"

Katrina laughed warmly. "This is our baby. I can't imagine wanting anything more," she said. She paused, taking a big breath. "Matthew, I was scared that you might not want this baby. At first I couldn't wrap my mind around you having a baby with someone else and me turning up pregnant, too. Then, when you showed up here, I was scared that you might not want children at all."

Matthew kissed her stomach a second time before he sat upright. "I want every one of our children, Katrina. And I also want us to be married when we have them, sweetheart. You need to know that I am totally committed to you and Collin, and this baby. I want us to be a family in every sense of the word. I love you. I love you with every ounce of my heart."

Katrina wrapped her arms around him and hugged him tightly. She held him close, not wanting to ever let him go. He loved her. He wanted her, her son and now their baby. Life couldn't have been sweeter, she thought as she told him that she loved him, too.

Chapter 23

Matthew and Katrina were just minutes away from landing at Phoenix Sky Harbor International Airport. As Matthew held her hand, caressing her fingers between his own, she marveled at how life could turn on a dime. A month or so ago she was convinced that everything she had trusted was lost to her. Even her faith in her own judgment had wavered, her usual instincts fragile. Just one week earlier she'd been pulling her hair out, trying to figure out the ramifications of her actions and the most responsible way for her to handle her pregnancy. And now, all was well, and the joy she felt was absolutely astounding.

Collin had been excited to hear that she and Matthew were on their way to take him back home to Dallas. Katrina could just imagine how the kid and her father had bumped heads during their brief time together, Collin's teenage angst and her dad's military austerity colliding like cold and warm fronts before a colossal storm. Neither of her parents had said a thing, but then they didn't need to. She was certain that her father, retired Master Sergeant Mason Boudreaux II, had things under complete control.

She was suddenly aware of Matthew staring at her, his intense gaze washing warmly over her. She smiled, meeting his intense stare. "What is it?" she questioned, curious.

He brushed the length of his fingers along the line of her profile. "You are incredibly beautiful," he said softly. He leaned over to kiss her cheek, sliding his arm around her shoulders as he pulled her close against him. "And I was just imagining how gorgeous our baby girl will be."

Katrina laughed. "Our baby girl? Are you wanting a daughter, Matthew Stallion?"

He laughed with her. "Sweetheart, I want whatever God blesses us with. But I admit to wanting to spoil a little girl, just like I plan to spoil her mother. And since we already have a son, I think a little girl would be very nice. What about you? Have you thought about whether or not you want a baby girl or a baby boy?"

A thoughtful look crossed Katrina's face. "No, I really haven't. As long as our baby is healthy, I will be perfectly happy."

"Healthy, happy, beautiful and a girl! I think that would be a winning combination." His grin was a mile wide.

"You're too cute," she responded, her own smile shining brightly. She leaned forward and wrapped her arms around his neck in a deep embrace, marveling once again at how quickly life had changed.

As their limousine maneuvered the circular driveway of the family's Paradise Valley estate, Mason Boudreaux III stepped out of the front entrance, his hand raised in greeting. His nephew Collin pushed past him excitedly, the boy jumping up and down as he waited for the vehicle to come to a halt.

Matthew gazed out the window, taking in the magnificent plantings and the rolling landscape of the forty-acre compound. The home sat high on Mummy Mountain, with panoramic views of the city and the mountains. Citrus trees lined the driveway and a breathtaking mountain view could be seen in the distance. "This is very nice!" he declared, nodding his approval.

"It's actually my brother's home. He built it and moved the old people in a few years ago. My father insists on doing the landscaping. It's become quite the hobby for him since the army retired him."

"What does your brother do?" Matthew asked.

Katrina smiled. "Mason owns a chain of hotels."

The car came to a stop, and Collin pulled the door open. His excited greeting echoed through the midday air. As Katrina stepped out of the car, the young man threw himself into her arms.

"When do we leave?" he asked. "I'm ready to go home."

Behind her, Matthew laughed. "Has it been that bad, kiddo?"

Collin rolled his eyes. "Worse! You just don't know!"

Katrina waved her head from side to side. She moved to her older brother's side and hugged him tightly. "Hey, you!"

Mason kissed her cheek and hugged her back. "Welcome home, kid!"

"It's good to be back, big brother." She reached for Matthew, gliding her arm around his waist. "Mason, I want you to meet Matthew Stallion. Matthew, this is my oldest brother, Mason Boudreaux the *third*."

Matthew stretched out his hand in greeting, taking note of the strong family resemblance between the siblings. "It's a pleasure."

"The pleasure is all mine, Matthew. Collin has been telling us all a lot about you."

"Don't hold that against me," Matthew said with a smile as he raked the boy's head with his fingers, Collin having moved to his side.

"I won't," Mason answered with a deep chuckle. "Come on inside, you two. Everybody's here," he said as he led them inside the large home.

Minutes later Matthew had been introduced to Katrina's large family: her mother, Katherine; sisters Tarah, Maitlyn and Kamaya; Kamaya's twin brother, Kendrick; and her brothers Donovan, Darryl and Guy. Lastly, he shook hands with the family patriarch, Mason Boudreaux II.

"Mr. Boudreaux, it's an honor to meet you, sir."

The elder Mason shook Matthew's extended hand, eyeing him from head to toe. "Everyone calls me Senior," he said. "My grandson speaks very highly of you."

"Your grandson is quite the young man."

"Boy has his moments," Senior answered. "I appreciate my daughter having someone with a firm hand to keep him in check. Boy his age can be a handful if you leave him unchecked."

"Your daughter does a wonderful job of doing that, sir. I think Katrina has a much firmer hand than I do."

The older man smiled ever so slightly as he wrapped his daughter in his arms and hugged her. He pressed a wet kiss against her cheek. "Baby girl was raised right," he said.

His wife giggled. "Matthew, don't pay that man no never mind. He was a big old teddy bear with his kids."

Senior laughed with her. "If you believe that, Mr. Stallion, I've got a bridge I'd like to sell you."

The whole family laughed.

"Collin, baby, take your mama's bags upstairs, please. Put them in the room where your aunt Tarah is staying. Put Mr. Stallion's bags in the room with you."

"Just a minute, Grandma," Collin responded.

Senior cleared his throat. "Your grandmother asked you to do it now, not in one minute. Get moving," the man admonished, his eyes narrowing into thin slits.

"Yes, sir," Collin mumbled, reaching for the luggage that had been dropped in the hallway.

Katrina laughed. "Don't buy the bridge, baby! Please don't buy the bridge!"

The family dynamics were so reminiscent of his own family's that Matthew had no problems feeling right at home. Laughter rang from one end of the massive home to the other, everyone regaling him with stories of their youth and Katrina's antics. He thoroughly enjoyed the time he spent in the kitchen with Katrina's mother as the woman directed him in the preparation of her famous mango salsa recipe, chiding him to chop the mangos, tomatoes, coriander leaves and chile peppers just so.

At one point Katrina stood in the doorway, staring, moving her mother to make a comment under her breath as she sidled up to Matthew at the counter. "My daughter's quite smitten with you, I see," she whispered, winking her eye.

Matthew cut an eye in Katrina's direction and smiled. He dropped his gaze back to the woman's. "I'm quite smitten with your daughter, Miss Katherine."

"I can see that. It's been a very long time since I've seen her so happy, and from what my other girls tell me, you're quite the catch."

Matthew laughed. "What else have they said about me, Miss Katherine?"

The woman smiled slyly. She hummed under her breath. "Mmm… Well…"

"Don't you dare say one word, Mama!" Katrina suddenly admonished, her face flushed with color.

Matthew's hearty chortle filled the room with warmth.

Katrina moved into the room and wrapped her arms around her mother's shoulders. "You're trying to start something, lady!"

"Yes, I am," Katherine said and laughed. She grabbed the

bowl of chopped vegetables from Matthew's hand and placed it in the refrigerator. "On a more serious note," she said as she moved back to the center island and changed the subject, "when do you plan to tell your father?"

Katrina cut her eye at Matthew and then back at her mother. "Tell him what?"

Katherine lowered her head slightly as she gazed up her daughter. "I'm not stupid, Katrina. I can see it in your face, and it doesn't help that Matthew is treating you like you might break at any moment. It's not for me to say, but you certainly need to tell you father before he finds out from someone else."

Katrina stammered, "I…we…it's…" She looked to Matthew for assistance.

Matthew drew a heavy palm against the small of her back. "I was waiting for the opportunity to speak with your husband first, Miss Katherine, before we make any formal announcements. Katrina and I are both very excited about the news we want to share with you. But out of respect for your family and your hospitality, it's only right that I have a man-to-man conversation with your husband first so that there are no misunderstandings about my intentions. I love your daughter very much, and it's important to me not only that you both trust that but that you think me worthy of her love."

Katherine studied him briefly, nodding her head ever so slightly. She reached out her arms to hug her daughter and then reached up on her toes to kiss Matthew's cheek. "I'm thinking my girls might be right about you, Matthew." She smiled sweetly. "Senior is out on the patio with Mason. If you'd ask my son to come give me a hand, please, I would appreciate it."

Matthew smiled. "Yes, ma'am," he said. He caressed Katrina's back one last time, then kissed her forehead before he made his way outside.

When the sliding glass doors were closed behind him and

he disappeared out of view, Katherine turned her gaze back to her daughter.

"I like that man, Katrina. I like that man very much."

She smiled at her mother, her head bobbing up and down. "I like him, too, Mama."

Katherine ran her hand across Katrina's abdomen, her eyebrows raised. "And I think he'll make a great father to my new grandbaby!"

There was a rush of noise behind them. "What grandbaby? Who's having a baby?" Katrina's sisters all chimed at the same time.

Tarah pressed her shoulder to Katrina's. "You are pregnant!" she exclaimed excitedly. "I knew it. I told Kamaya that glow was about something else other than that man."

"Yes, she did," Kamaya said as she rinsed her hands in the sink and reached for a paper towel.

"Although a man that fine could make a woman glow and then some," Maitlyn murmured loudly as she peeked out the window. "So, does he have brothers?" she asked as she leaned over the counter, reaching for a carrot stick.

Katrina laughed. "He has three of them but they're all taken."

Tarah waved her hand at Maitlyn. "Do you ever think about anything besides men? Our sister is having another baby, and you're distracted by a man just like that."

"Didn't a man get her pregnant?" Maitlyn countered. "And I don't always think about men. In fact the only thing on my mind right now is how to get rid of the lying, cheating man I'm married to."

Katrina wrapped her arms around her sister's shoulder. "I was sorry to hear about you and Don breaking up. I was hoping you two could work it out."

Maitlyn shrugged. "You can't work things out with a man who is not interested in being in a relationship with you. It's better we split amicably before it gets any uglier."

Their mother grunted, her annoyance painting her expression. It was on the tip of the matriarch's tongue to tell her daughter that she had told her so when Tarah interrupted before the older woman could say anything.

"Um, excuse me... Off subject...again. How did you get pregnant?" Tarah asked, turning her attention back to Katrina.

The other women laughed.

Kamaya shook her head. "That man!" she exclaimed, chuckling heartily.

Katrina laughed with them, rolling her eyes skyward. "It definitely wasn't planned," she revealed, as she filled her family in on everything that had happened with her and Matthew since they'd met.

"Wow!" Kamaya exclaimed when she was done.

"Double wow!" Maitlyn added. "Paris? Really?"

"I'm still blown away about the football stadium," Tarah said.

Katrina was nodding her head in agreement. "Everything he does is just big and over the top."

"Your brother Mason has gotten that way," Kamaya said. "He's become quite the romantic with the ladies! I keep telling Kendrick he needs to take lessons."

Katherine smiled. She gestured with the knife in her hand, shaking it in both of her daughters' direction. "All of my boys are romantic in their own way. It doesn't take a whole lot of flashy money for a man to show his interest in a woman. You girls know that."

"It's not about the money, Mama," Katrina said, nodding her head in agreement. "Yes, his wealth makes it easy for him to do things others might not be able to do, but it's so much more. He's creative and attentive and compassionate and—" she paused, her gaze drifting out to where she knew Matthew was deep in conversation with her father "—and he loves me and he loves Collin. He's just... He's—"

Maitlyn interrupted. "He's special," she said teasingly, her eyes widened in amusement.

The sisters laughed.

Katrina's head waved from side to side. "Yes, he is," she said. "Yes, he is."

"Well, Senior looks like he's about to choke Mr. Special," Tarah said, staring out the window to where her father and Matthew stood. She slowly eased up the window, hoping to hear what was being said.

"What are you doing, young lady?" her mother admonished, moving to stare where she stared.

"Being nosy," Tarah answered as she stepped closer to the window.

The rest of the Boudreaux women gathered around them.

"This might not be a good idea," Katrina said.

Kamaya pressed her index finger to her lips. "Shhh," she whispered as they all leaned forward to hear. And that was when they heard Matthew tell their father that he wanted to marry Katrina.

In the twin bed on the other side of the room Collin snored softly. Matthew sat upright in his own bed, pulling his knees up to his chest as he leaned back against the pillows. The two of them had talked for hours, Collin catching him up on all that he had been doing since arriving in Arizona. Matthew had liked how the young man had sought out his opinion about a young lady he was smitten with, about his progress at the ranch and about whether or not he should spend his summer savings on the newest Nike basketball sneakers. They had also had a conversation about Matthew marrying his mother and about the new little brother or sister that would be coming.

Matthew knew that Collin's nonchalant attitude was probably just the quiet before a typical teenage storm, but he was also aware that honesty and open lines of communica-

Seduced by a Stallion

tion would be the key to their becoming a united family unit. Katrina had been nervous about sharing their news with her son, but Matthew knew the sooner they included him, and the rest of the family, the better off they would all be.

Matthew reflected back on his own conversation with Katrina's father. Mason and his namesake, Mason III, had been in deep conversation when Matthew stepped out on the back patio. He'd been reluctant to interrupt them, but when Mason saw him standing there, he'd drawn him into the conversation.

"Matthew, my father and I were just discussing the hotel business. Come join us."

Matthew smiled. "I don't know that I can be of any help to you, Mason. My family has diversified in a number of directions, but hotel operations isn't one of them."

"Do you think it's something you and your brothers might consider?" Mason asked.

Matthew shrugged. "Anything is possible. What are you suggesting?"

"I was just telling my father that I think it's time for a changing of the guard at Boudreaux International. I'm looking to do something different with my life. I haven't truly been challenged in the past few years, and I'm starting to feel it."

Matthew nodded, his mind skating over the possibilities. "Let's talk more later," he said. Then he relayed Katherine's message to her oldest son. The three men were amused by her insistence when just minutes later she stuck her head out the door and reiterated her demand.

"Mason, what part of 'come help me' didn't you understand?" Katherine scolded, her crooked finger beckoning him inside.

"You've been called, son," Senior observed with a chuckle. "Better step to it!"

Mason rolled his eyes skyward, his head waving from side to side. "Gentlemen, if you'll excuse me," he said, heading in his mother's direction.

Senior nodded his approval, still chuckling as Matthew moved into the seat that had just been vacated.

"Mr. Boudreaux, sir—"

The patriarch interrupted him. "Son, Mr. Boudreaux was my father and I was named after him. Everyone called me Junior right up to the day my father passed on and my son Mason was born. Since then everyone has called me Senior. Everyone," he explained, the decisiveness of his tone commanding.

Matthew smiled. "Yes, sir," he responded. "I was hoping that we could speak privately for a minute."

Senior leaned forward in his seat. "Is here okay, or would you prefer we go inside to my office?"

"This is just fine, sir."

"Go on then."

"Senior," Matthew began, then cleared his throat. He took a deep breath and continued. "I am sure that you're aware that I am very fond of your daughter. Katrina and I have become exceptionally close over the past few months, and, sir…" He paused. "I've asked her to be my wife.

"Our families mean a lot to both of us, and it's important to Katrina and to me that we have your support, and your approval." Matthew exhaled and then took a second breath. "Most especially since we're also expecting a baby. Katrina is pregnant with my child."

Matthew's declaration was met with Senior's blank expression, the man staring at Matthew intently. Minutes passed before the patriarch responded.

"So, what you're telling me is you're only marrying my daughter because she's pregnant?"

Aghast, Matthew shook his head profusely. "Oh, no, sir, not at all. I proposed to Katrina well before she told me about the baby. I love your daughter. I love her with every fiber of my soul. There is nothing I wouldn't do or give to ensure her future happiness. I want to marry your daughter because I want to spend the rest of my life with her."

There was another lengthy pause before the old man spoke. "Well, you two are doing this thing backward, but at least you're doing it. And it's not like you and Katrina are seventeen, either. I was not happy about Katrina marrying as early as she did that first time, but she and her first husband proved me and her mother wrong. Collin's father made her very happy, and that made me happy. I haven't seen her smile like that in a very long time. Not until today, when she brought you home for us to meet." Senior heaved a deep sigh. "It looks like my daughter loves you as much as you would seem to love her."

Rising to his feet, he extended his hand in Matthew's direction. Matthew came to his own feet, and the two men shook hands.

"You both have my blessing. Take care of my baby girl, and we won't have any problems between us. Welcome to the family, son."

From the kitchen window, the Boudreaux women all shouted with glee, their excitement spilling out into the afternoon air. Katrina came rushing out the sliding glass doors, throwing herself against Matthew. Her mother followed on her heels, moving into her husband's arms.

Senior shook his head, his gaze meeting Matthew's evenly. "Son, now, can you just imagine what they would have done had I said no?"

Collin rolling onto his side, mumbling softly in his sleep, drew Matthew back to the moment. In the darkness, he stared toward where the boy tossed and turned until he slipped back into a sound sleep. Matthew smiled as the memory of the experience warmed his spirit. He knew that he and Katrina were headed in the right direction. He couldn't wait till they got to their future. Settling down in the bed, he pulled the sheet up over his body, rolled over onto his side and drifted off into the sweetest sleep.

Chapter 24

The noise emanating from the family room at the ranch had risen ten decibels since the Stallion women had commandeered Katrina for a female powwow about her and Matthew's wedding plans. Stuffed from the breakfast they'd just eaten, Matthew and his brothers had retreated into the home's study as they tried to stay out of the line of fire.

John interrupted Mark and Luke's conversation, the two men analyzing the pending game between the Cowboys and the Steelers. "I've reviewed the initial portfolio, and Boudreaux International would appear to be a very worthy acquisition."

Matthew nodded. "I like what I've read so far, as well, and I've got my team going through all their legal agreements to see where we would stand."

"So, we're going into the hotel business?" Luke asked. He reclined on the leather office sofa, his legs crossed at the ankles over the sofa's arm.

John and Matthew both looked in his direction and shrugged. "We still have a lot of research to do," John answered.

"Oh, yeah!" Luke exclaimed. "That's what I'm talking about! Research in the lap of luxury. Joanne and I are going to have a good time! I think I should start hotel hopping right away. I mean, Boudreaux International has forty-five hundred hotels in over one hundred countries, and you know we'll need to visit each and every one."

John rolled his eyes, his head shaking. "Uh, no. This is not fun and games time for you and your girl. This is business. And I taught you better. But I am impressed, little brother, that you've been doing your homework."

Luke laughed, snapping his fingers in jest. "Awww, shucks! Oh, well, I'll just have to have that good time without her."

"Don't say it," Mark said with a chuckle, his gaze meeting John's. "He's still a pup. You know he's going to have to learn his lesson the hard way."

John's head waved from side to side. He had to laugh at his baby brother's frivolity, the youngest of them never seeming to take anything seriously, despite his division posting some of the best profits in the company's history. "If I were you, Luke, I wouldn't count on my good time just yet. There's still a lot of work that needs to be accomplished before we start thinking about site visits."

Matthew interjected, "Katrina's brother says we can have full access to whatever information we need. He's ready to do this."

John nodded. "How soon can we set up a face-to-face with him?"

"Whenever you want," Matthew answered. "Just let me know when you're ready." He glanced down at the watch on his wrist. "Meanwhile, good buddies, I need to rescue my girl."

John laughed. "You can see your wedding budget blowing up already, can't you?"

Matthew laughed. "You just don't know!"

Heading into the family room, Matthew found himself smack-dab in the middle of a conversation about bridal gowns.

"I'm a big Maggie Sottero fan," Joanne was saying. "Love, love, love her gowns!"

"And Pronovias!" Marah exclaimed. "You'd look great in a Pronovias gown," she said, typing on the laptop computer that sat in front of them. "See," she said, turning the screen toward Katrina.

"Oh, they are beautiful!" Katrina gushed.

"My baby could wear a potato sack and look beautiful," Matthew interjected as he planted a kiss against Katrina's neck.

She smiled, blushing profusely at the attention. "I may need a potato sack," she said, patting the slight curve of her pregnant belly.

"If you really want to go that route, I probably have one or two that you can borrow," Michelle said as she scooped baby Irene to her shoulder, nuzzling her chin against her daughter's forehead. She chuckled softly.

Katrina laughed, admiring how serenely the infant slept against her mother. The birth of baby Irene had awakened her longing to hold the child that was growing inside of her. Matthew was thinking the same thing as he gently squeezed Katrina's shoulder.

They had arrived back in Dallas just in time to make it to the hospital for the baby's birth. Mark had been petrified as they'd whisked him back to the delivery room to see his daughter being born. Spying his brother Matthew just seconds before disappearing behind one of the nurses had been a great comfort to him.

As always the entire Stallion clan had been gathered, excited to welcome the new member of their growing family. Both Katrina and Collin noted that it felt as if they were still home with family in Arizona. Both loved how that felt.

Vanessa had been front and center to welcome them home. Without a moment's hesitation she passed Vaughan to Matthew and wrapped her thin arms around Katrina's torso. "It's about time you reeled him in," she'd whispered into Katrina's ear. "I'm Vanessa and the kid there is Vaughan."

"It's nice to officially meet you, Vanessa," Katrina had said, a wide smile pulling at her mouth. "And I'm glad you didn't name him Matt-lena. That would not have been pretty," she had whispered back.

Vanessa had laughed heartily. "You are so right!" she'd exclaimed.

When little Irene had been delivered safely, both mother and child given a clean bill of health, the whole family had rejoiced. As they'd stood outside the maternity window, eyeing the beautiful bundle cradled securely in Mark's arms, Matthew hadn't been able to wait to add to the celebration.

"Katrina and I are having a baby, too!" he'd gushed, pulling her into his arms. "And we're getting married!"

The whole family had roared with glee, and behind the glass window, Mark had grinned like a Cheshire cat, giving his big brother a big thumbs-up.

Matthew squeezed Katrina's shoulder a second time. "Ladies, I need to steal my fiancée away for a while," he said. "But you ladies keep at it."

Katrina eyed him curiously as he entwined his fingers with hers and pulled her out of her seat. "Where are we going?" she asked, her eyes skating over his coy expression.

Knowing that each ear in the room had perked up at her question, Matthew said nothing, just shrugging his shoulders as he guided her out of the room, to the front foyer and out of the house. At the foot of the wide front steps a large four-wheeler sat in wait. Katrina tossed him a questioning look, a wave of confusion washing over her. Matthew turned to give her a seductive smile, still not uttering a word. He climbed on board and held out his hand to help her climb atop.

"Is this safe?" Katrina asked, skepticism flooding her tone.

"Would I ever put you in harm's way?" Matthew answered. He reached for her arms and pulled them around his waist, clasping her hands together in front of him. "Hold on tight," he commanded as he started the engine.

Katrina laughed into his ear. "You do not have to worry about that," she said as they headed toward the edge of the estate, disappearing into the line of trees that skirted the property. As Matthew guided them deeper and deeper into the brush, Katrina wasn't sure what to think about this impromptu excursion.

Minutes later the trees parted and Katrina found herself in a clearing, the likes of which took her breath away. The grassy knoll had a plethora of blooming flowers that surrounded a small pond with a cascading waterfall. It was nirvana, and her delight with it was evident all over her face.

"This is beautiful!" she cooed, brushing her palms across his chest. "Absolutely beautiful!"

Matthew helped her off the vehicle, guiding her to the water's edge. He pulled a blanket from the back pocket of the passenger seat, easing it under his arm. She held his hand as they took a short stroll. As Katrina stood staring out over the water, Matthew spread the blanket across the ground. Then he moved to her side and wrapped his arms around her torso as she leaned back against him, taking in the magnificent view.

"I just wanted you all to myself for a minute," he said as his hand glided across her abdomen. "All to myself," he repeated. He nuzzled his face into her hair, inhaling the sweet scent of coconut oil along the strands.

They stood together for some time, both enamored with the view and each other, imagining the possibilities that lay ahead for them. Spinning around in his arms, Katrina clutched the front of his shirt as she leaned up to kiss his mouth. He tasted sweet, like the pineapple juice he'd had for breakfast. When he parted her lips with his tongue, easing into her mouth, the sensation shot through her as if an explosive device had been detonated with full force. Gliding her hand over the front of him, she could feel that he had hardened in his pants, an erection pressing urgently between them. The explosion had rocked them both.

"Can anyone see us?" she asked, pulling away from him.

Matthew shrugged. "No, I wouldn't think so. I don't expect that anyone will even know we're here," he said.

The smile on Katrina's face was wicked as she took a step back. She slowly pushed one strap of her sundress off her shoulder. Matthew eyed her hungrily as she slowly pushed the other strap down, allowing the garment to fall to the ground at her feet. She stood naked before him, wearing nothing but a black G-string, and then that was tossed to the ground.

He cupped his palm over his crotch, his manhood feeling as if it were ready to convulse with pleasure. The look in his eye was one of pure hunger. Had there been a roof above their heads, his pulse and heart rate would have shot through it. It was enough that there was a knot in his throat and it wasn't going away.

She stepped to him, her body so close to his that he could hear her breathing. Sliding one hand behind his neck, she pulled him down to her and kissed him again, capturing his lips with reckless abandon. She shivered uncontrollably when Matthew dropped both hands to her hips, gliding her body against his own.

Anxious to feel his bare flesh against hers, Katrina began to unbutton his shirt and then his pants, pulling frantically until he was free from his clothes. She kissed him again, gently at first, and then she opened her mouth to him, her tongue dancing excitedly with his. Matthew clutched the back of her neck and deepened the kiss even further.

Easing her down to the blanket, Matthew kissed her neck, nibbling gently at her flesh. Katrina moaned her pleasure into the midday air, the sound of it blowing in the warm breeze. She savored every moment of his touch as he glided his hands up and down the length of her body.

Lying back, Matthew shifted until Katrina was lying on top of him. He reclaimed her lips, one hand tangled in her hair, the other clutching the round of her butt cheeks. Katrina moaned at the skin-on-skin contact. Easing his fingers between her legs, he pushed them into her, administering to the bundle of swollen flesh that pulsed there. It was almost too much to bear as Katrina fell into a trance of sheer pleasure. She gyrated her hips, grinding her pelvis against his hand.

"Oh, ohh, ohhh," she moaned over and over again.

Sitting upright, Matthew flipped her onto her back and slid his body into hers, dipping into the puddle of wetness that had pooled between her thighs. His strokes were long and slow as he caressed her inner lining with the length of himself. Their loving was like nothing either of them had ever experienced before, as magnificent as if they were experiencing each other for the very first time. Matthew captured her mouth one more time, his own pleasure washing through him in deep waves.

When he could feel Katrina sliding toward the edge, beginning to convulse around him, his own orgasm suddenly ripped through him. She chanted his name. "Matthew! Oh, Matthew! I'm… I'm coming…" she cried, tears of joy washing past her lashes. Her words melted into an incoherent jumble.

"That's it, baby. Let it go, darling," he answered, spasms rippling through every muscle in his body. They were both swept up into pure sensation, feeling the open air and hearing the sound of the waterfall through every fiber of their being.

When Matthew finally collapsed above her, both of them were spent with exhaustion. They lay side by side for some time, trading gentle caresses and light kisses as the sun rose high in the brilliantly blue sky.

Katrina lifted herself up on an elbow to look down at him.

"Will it always be this way, Matthew?" she asked. "Do you promise to always bring that Stallion heat?"

He smiled sweetly, nodding his head ever so gently. "For the rest of our lives, my love. For the rest of our lives."

Katrina smiled back. "I love you!" she said, draping her body over his. "I love you so much!"

Matthew Stallion kissed her gently, holding her tightly to him. "I love you, too!"

* * * * *

REQUEST YOUR FREE BOOKS!

2 FREE NOVELS
PLUS 2 FREE GIFTS!

KIMANI™
ROMANCE

Love's ultimate destination!

YES! Please send me 2 FREE Kimani™ Romance novels and my 2 FREE gifts (gifts are worth about $10). After receiving them, if I don't wish to receive any more books, I can return the shipping statement marked "cancel." If I don't cancel, I will receive 4 brand-new novels every month and be billed just $4.94 per book in the U.S. or $5.49 per book in Canada. That's a saving of at least 21% off the cover price. It's quite a bargain! Shipping and handling is just 50¢ per book in the U.S. and 75¢ per book in Canada.* I understand that accepting the 2 free books and gifts places me under no obligation to buy anything. I can always return a shipment and cancel at any time. Even if I never buy another book, the two free books and gifts are mine to keep forever.

168/368 XDN FEJR

Name	(PLEASE PRINT)	
Address		Apt. #
City	State/Prov.	Zip/Postal Code

Signature (if under 18, a parent or guardian must sign)

Mail to the **Reader Service:**
IN U.S.A.: P.O. Box 1867, Buffalo, NY 14240-1867
IN CANADA: P.O. Box 609, Fort Erie, Ontario L2A 5X3

Not valid for current subscribers to Kimani Romance books.

Want to try two free books from another line?
Call 1-800-873-8635 or visit www.ReaderService.com.

* Terms and prices subject to change without notice. Prices do not include applicable taxes. Sales tax applicable in N.Y. Canadian residents will be charged applicable taxes. Offer not valid in Quebec. This offer is limited to one order per household. All orders subject to credit approval. Credit or debit balances in a customer's account(s) may be offset by any other outstanding balance owed by or to the customer. Please allow 4 to 6 weeks for delivery. Offer available while quantities last.

Your Privacy—The Reader Service is committed to protecting your privacy. Our Privacy Policy is available online at www.ReaderService.com or upon request from the Reader Service.

We make a portion of our mailing list available to reputable third parties that offer products we believe may interest you. If you prefer that we not exchange your name with third parties, or if you wish to clarify or modify your communication preferences, please visit us at www.ReaderService.com/consumerschoice or write to us at Reader Service Preference Service, P.O. Box 9062, Buffalo, NY 14269. Include your complete name and address.

KROM11B

31901051357921